CHRISTMAS IN THE
BOSS'S CASTLE

CHRISTMAS IN THE BOSS'S CASTLE

BY

SCARLET WILSON

MILLS & BOON

First published in Great Britain 2016
By Mills & Boon, an imprint of HarperCollins*Publishers*
1 London Bridge Street, London, SE1 9GF

Large Print edition 2017

© 2016 Harlequin Books S.A.

Special thanks and acknowledgment are given to
Scarlet Wilson for her contribution to the Maids Under the
Mistletoe series.

ISBN: 978-0-263-07084-2

This book is dedicated
my favourite little people,
Taylor Hyndman, Noah 'Batman' Dickson,
Lleyton Hyndman and Luca Dickson.
Let's hope you're all on Santa's 'nice' list this year!

CHAPTER ONE

GRACE BRUSHED THE snow from her shoulders as she ducked in the back door of the exclusive Armstrong hotel in Chelsea, London. It was just after six in the morning, the streets were still dark and she could see her footprints in the snow outside.

Frank, the senior concierge, came in behind her. A wide grin lit up his face as he saw her looking at the snow outside. 'Finally,' he muttered as he shook the snow from his coat and started to sing the words to *It's Beginning To Look A Lot Like Christmas*. The words of the song floated from his lips. He gave her a nudge. 'You're too young to remember this one.'

She raised her eyebrows. 'Frank, you should know, I know every version of every Christmas song that's ever existed.'

They walked into the changing room. 'What version do you want to go for? Johnny Mathis, Frank Sinatra, or Michael Buble?' She started singing alongside him as she wound her long brown hair up into a loose bun and tied on her white chambermaid's apron over her black shirt and skirt.

Christmas was her absolute favourite time of year. It brought back great memories of the Christmases she'd spent with her grandmother in the little flat they'd shared in one of the poorer parts of London. But what they didn't have in wealth, they'd certainly made up for in love. This would be her first Christmas without her gran and she was determined not to be sad and gloomy—her gran would never have wanted that for her.

Frank slid his arms into his dark green and gold jacket and started fastening the buttons. 'I swear this thing shrinks every night when I put it into my locker.'

Grace laughed and closed her locker, walking over to Frank and pulling his jacket a little closer across his wide girth, helping him with the buttons. He kept singing the whole time. She finished with a sigh. 'I wish those words were true.'

Frank frowned as he glanced at his reflection in the nearby mirror and straightened his jacket. They started walking down the lower corridor of the hotel together. She shrugged. 'I wish it was beginning to look a lot like Christmas.' She held out her hands. 'Because it certainly isn't in here.' She gave a shake of her head. 'I don't get it. All the other big hotels in London have huge Christmas trees in their reception area and garlands and holly wreaths everywhere.'

The Armstrong hotel was part of a luxurious chain across the world. Locations in London, Paris, Tokyo, Rome and New York were regularly used by statesmen, politicians, rock stars and Hollywood celebrities. They were the epitome of glamour, renowned for their exclusivity, personal touches and attention to detail. It was a far cry from the small flat that Grace lived in and over the past few months she'd secretly loved seeing how the other half lived their lives. She knew one pop star that never laundered their underwear and instead just threw them away. A politician who had a secret interest in romance novels and a statesman that only ate red-coloured candy.

They reached the stairway up to the main reception. Frank held the door open for her and pressed his lips together. But now Grace had started, she couldn't stop. 'I mean, I know this place is exclusive, but the minimalist Christmas decorations?' She gave another shake of her head. 'They just look—well…cold.'

Frank sighed as he headed over towards his granite-topped desk. He spoke quietly as he glanced around the reception area. Everything was sleek and shades of black or grey. 'I know.' His eyes took in the small black and glass sign on the main reception desk.

The Armstrong wishes you
a Merry Christmas.

It was the only concession to Christmas on show. He checked the ledger on the desk in front of him and handed Grace an envelope. 'The Armstrong used to have beautiful Christmas decorations and lights. All exclusive. All extortionate. But they added colour to the place. Vibrancy.'

Grace started to automatically open the envelope with her day's assignments. She glanced upwards. 'So, what happened?'

Frank paused for a second before finally answering. Her gaze narrowed. Although she'd only been working here a few months, Frank had been here for ever. He was thoroughly professional, good at his job and for the guests who returned time after time—a most welcome sight. 'They had a rebranding,' he said finally.

Grace frowned. She wanted to ask more, but, like most good concierges, Frank had always been the soul of discretion. It was unlikely she'd get any more out of him.

She waved her assignment at him. 'I wish they'd let me do the rebranding around here. I could sprinkle some Christmas fairy dust.' She held out her hands and spun around. 'Some silver lights up here, some red ones over there. A tree near the glass doors. How about some garlands at the reception desk? And a huge pile of beautifully wrapped presents in the little alcove, just as you go through to the bar.' She stopped spinning, closed her eyes and held her hands to her chest. For a few seconds she could actually see in her head what this place could look like. The welcome. The warmth. The festivities.

Frank let out a wry laugh. 'Keep dreaming, Grace.'

Her eyelids flickered back open. Grey. Sleek. Blackness everywhere. She leaned forward across Frank's desk. 'I could even make this place *smell* like Christmas. Cookies. Cinnamon sticks. Cranberries. Pine trees and Christmas spices. And *not* from some tacky candle.'

Frank arched an eyebrow and leaned over towards her. 'There's a lot to be said for candles. And I'm sure we've got a whole host of those things packed up in the basement somewhere.' He shook his head. 'But I doubt very much we'll ever see them again.' He gave her a careful nod. 'You should take some home with you. Make good use of them.'

She gave a half-smile. He knew. He'd heard from some of the other girls that she was on her own. Grace didn't like people feeling sorry for her. But Frank had only the best of intentions. She knew that. So, she couldn't be offended by his good intentions. In fact, she was quite sure that some time, some place he might actually dress up as Santa.

Truth was, while The Armstrong hotel was opulent, its biggest asset was actually the staff. There were no 'bad pennies' as her gran used to call them.

Everything here was luxurious. From the bed sheets, to the furnishings, the Michelin-starred restaurant, even the heavy-duty stationery that her daily work assignment was printed on.

It was a world away from what she'd been brought up in. Working with the Maids in Chelsea agency had been a blessing in disguise. When her grandmother had died almost a year ago after a long battle with cancer, Grace had realised it was time to stop putting her own life on hold. Her gran had been the biggest part of her world. For a few years she'd only managed to take temporary part-time jobs that fitted in around being full-time carer for her gran. Working as a chambermaid might not be many women's dream job, but the salary was good and her work colleagues had turned into the best bunch of friends a girl could have.

As it was one of London's exclusive hotels, work at The Armstrong varied. There were a few guests that stayed here permanently. Some of the city's big businesses always had rooms on hold for their overseas visitors. A few of the suites seemed to be permanently vacant. Then, there were the celebrity guests.

In the space of a few months Grace had seen enough scandal and impropriety to keep the tabloid presses in headlines for the next year. But confidentiality was part of the contract for Maids in Chelsea—and she would never have breathed a word anyway.

Today's assignment was a little different. She headed over to the reception desk. 'Anya, can I just check? I've to clean the Nottingdale Suite? The penthouse? No one has stayed there in the whole time I've worked here.'

Anya checked the computer system. 'Yes, it's going to be used later. We're expecting the guest around five.'

'Who normally stays there?'

Anya smiled. 'I'm not sure. I did hear a rumour it was the reclusive tycoon who owns the whole chain.'

Grace tried not to let her mouth hang open. 'Really? Is it a man or a woman? What's their name?'

Anya held up her hands. 'You tell me. You've worked here longer than I have.'

Grace shook her head. 'I haven't paid that much attention. And I've never been in the penthouse.' She winked at Anya. 'This could be fun.'

The morning flew past. And it was fun. She cleaned a few rooms. Made a few special request orders for guests. Unpacked seven giant cases for a guest who was staying for only two nights. Then spent nearly an hour with Mrs Alice Archer, her favourite long-term guest who was eighty-nine going on twenty-one. Mrs Archer needed special soft sheets for her bed due to a long-term skin condition that affected her back, legs and arms. Grace was happy to give her a hand applying cream to spots she couldn't quite reach and helping her into whatever fabulous outfit she'd picked for the day. Alice's walk-in wardrobe was every girl's fantasy. It was full of original nineteen-forties clothes—all completely immaculate. Gorgeous full skirts, waist-cinching jackets, gingham dresses, a rainbow array of neckerchiefs, fitted sweaters and a few rarely worn satin evening gowns. There were a handbag and shoes to match every outfit.

Alice Archer had her hair styled twice a week, was fastidious with her make-up, favouring bright red lipstick, and drank lemon tea that Grace prepared for her most mornings, once she'd been helped into her clothes. In a way she reminded Grace of her grandmother. Oh, her grandmother had certainly never had the lifestyle that Alice had experienced. But both had the same quick wit, sharp minds and big hearts. Grace finished fastening Alice's shoes as she sipped her lemon tea.

'What are you doing today? Lunch or afternoon tea?'

Alice patted her hand. 'Thank you, Grace. It's Thursday. So it's afternoon tea at the Ritz. I'm meeting an old colleague.' She nudged Grace. 'He proposed to me once, you know.'

Grace looked up. 'He did? Now that sounds interesting. Why didn't you marry him?'

Alice let out a laugh. 'Harry? Not a chance. Harry was a cad. A man about town. He would have broken my heart. So I had to break his first.'

Grace blinked. It was the throwaway way that she said it. There was a trace of something else behind those carefully made-up eyes. Did Alice regret her choice?

She hoped not. A man about town. Definitely not the type of guy that Grace was looking for. She'd never want a relationship with a man who only wanted a fling, or something meaningless. She'd suffered rejection enough. It was pretty much the worst thing in the world to be abandoned by your mother; hers had moved to another continent, married another man and created the family she'd really wanted, instead of the unexpected teenage pregnancy she'd ended up with.

Grace had always been determined that would never be her. She wasn't prepared to hand her heart over to anyone. Least of all a man that wouldn't value and respect her. She wanted everything: the knight on the white horse, the total commitment and someone with eyes only for her.

Hence the reason she was still on her own.

She rested back on her heels and looked up at Alice. 'Well, I'm sure that you couldn't have broken his heart too much, or all these years later he wouldn't still be meeting you.'

Alice sighed and leaned back in her chair. 'Or maybe we're the only ones left,' she said wistfully. Grace reached up and put her hand over Alice's frail one, giving it a gentle squeeze. 'I bet he'll be delighted to see you.'

After a second Alice seemed to snap out of her thoughts. 'What do you have planned? Tell me you've finally decided it's time to say yes to one of those nice young men that keep asking you out.'

Grace felt her cheeks flush. Alice's favourite hobby seemed to be trying to pair her off with a 'suitable' young man. She wasn't quite sure any of the men that had asked her out recently would be Alice's definition of suitable though. Lenny, the biker, had been looking for somewhere cheap to stay and thought asking Grace out might solve his problems. Alan, the banker, had earned another nickname in her head—as soon as darkness had surrounded them he'd turned into the eight-handed octopus. Ross from college had merely been looking for someone who might do the shopping and make him dinner. And Nathan? He'd seemed perfect. Handsome, hard-working and endearingly polite. But when he'd leaned in for that first kiss they'd both realised there was absolutely no spark.

She was still searching for her knight on a white horse.

In a way it made her sad. Her friends at Maids in Chelsea seemed to be pairing off at an alarming rate. Emma had just reunited with Jack—the husband nobody had known she had. Ashleigh seemed to have fallen under the spell of her gorgeous Greek, Lukas. Even Clio, their boss, had just announced her engagement to her old boyfriend Enrique and was currently planning an intimate New Year wedding. Then two nights ago her fellow singleton Sophie had mysteriously disappeared. Grace was beginning to feel like the inevitable spare part.

She shook her head at Alice and stood up. 'No men for me, I'm afraid. Maybe we can make a New Year's resolution together to try and find some suitable beaus.'

Alice let out a laugh. 'Now, that would be fun.' She glanced at the clock. 'What are you doing next?'

Grace glanced at the clock too and gave a start. Where had the time gone? 'Oh, I'll have to rush. I'm going to make up the penthouse suite—the Nottingdale. I've never even been in it before. I heard it belongs to the owner.'

Alice stared at her for a second with her bright blue eyes.

'What? Do you know him? Or her?'

Alice pressed her lips together. She seemed hesitant to speak. Finally she gave a little smile. 'I've stayed here a while. I might know *him* a little.'

Grace grinned. She was instantly intrigued. 'Go on, then. Tell me about him. He's a bit mysterious. No one seems to know much about him.'

Alice shook her head. 'Oh, no, Grace. Sometimes mystery is good. I'm sure you'll meet him in good time.'

Grace narrowed her eyes good-naturedly as she headed towards the door. 'Alice Archer, I get the distinct impression you could tell me more.' She shook her head. 'But I'd better get on. Have fun with your afternoon tea.'

She closed the door behind her and took out her staff key for the elevator to the penthouse.

The elevator didn't just move. It glided. Like something out of the space age. It made her want to laugh. The rest of the hotel used the original elevators and Grace actually loved them. The little padded velvet love seat in the back, the panelled wood interior and the large brass button display inside. This private elevator was much like the front entrance. Shades of smooth black and grey. So silent that even her breathing seemed to disturb the air. When the doors slid open she almost jumped.

She stepped outside pulling her little trolley behind her. The entrance to the penthouse was different from the rest of the hotel. Usually the way to guest rooms was lined with thick carpet. The entrance way here was tiled, making the noise of the trolley bumping from the elevator echo all around her.

There was a huge black solid door in front of her with a pristine glass sign to its right: 'The Nottingdale Suite'.

She swallowed. Her mouth felt dry. It was ridiculous. She was nervous. About what?

She slid her staff card into the locking mechanism at the door. An electronic voice broke the silence. *Grace Ellis, Housekeeping.* She let out a shriek and looked around. In the last few months that had never happened anywhere in the hotel. It took a few seconds for her heart to stop clambering against her chest. Her card had actually identified her?

She pulled it out and stared at it for a second. Her befuddled brain started swirling. Of course, her staff card probably identified everywhere she went in the hotel. That was why she had it. But it had never actually said her name out loud before. There was something quite unnerving about that. Something a little too futuristic.

Hesitantly, she pushed open the door. It swung back easily and she drew in a breath. Straight in front of her were the biggest windows she'd ever seen, displaying the whole of Chelsea—and lots of London beyond around them. Her feet moved automatically until her breath misted the glass. The view was spectacular.

Kings Road with its array of exquisite shops, Sloane Square. If she looked in the other direction she could see the Chelsea embankment with Battersea Park on the other side and Albert Bridge. The view at night when everything was lit up must be spectacular.

Beneath her were rows of beautiful white Georgian town houses, mews cottages, streets lined with cherry trees. Houses filled with celebrities, Russian oligarchs and international businessmen. Security at all these houses probably cost more than she earned in a year.

She spun around and began to tour the penthouse. The still air was disturbing. Almost as if no one had been in here for a long time. But the bedroom held a large dark travel case. Someone had been here. If only to drop off the luggage.

She looked around. The bed was bare—waiting to be made up. It took her a few minutes to find the bedding—concealed inside a black gloss cupboard that sprang open as she pressed her fingertips against it. It only took a few minutes to make up the bed with the monochrome bedding.

Underneath her fingertips she could feel the quality but the effect still left her cold.

She opened the case and methodically unpacked the clothing. It all belonged to a man. Polished handmade shoes. Italian cut suits. Made-to-measure shirts. She was almost finished when she felt a little lump inside the case. It only took a second to realise the lump was from something hidden in an inside pocket.

She pulled out the wad of tissue paper and unwrapped it carefully as she sat on the bed. The tissue paper felt old—as if it had wrapped this item for a number of years. By the time she finally peeled back the last layer she sucked in her breath.

It was gorgeous. A sparkling Christmas angel, delicately made from ceramic. Easily breakable—no wonder it was wrapped so carefully. She held it up by the string, letting it dangle in the afternoon light. Even though it was mainly white, the gold and silver glitter gave it warmth. It was a beautiful Christmas tree ornament. One that should be decorating a tree in someone's house, not being hidden in the pocket in a case.

Her heart gave a little start as she looked around the room. Maybe this businessman was having to spend his Christmas apart from his family? Maybe this was the one thing that gave him a little hint of home?

She looked around the cold, sleek room as ideas started to spark in her brain. Frank had told there were decorations in the basement. Maybe she could make this room a little more welcoming? A little bit more like Christmas?

Her smile spread from ear to ear as her spirits lifted a little. She didn't want to be lonely this Christmas. She certainly didn't want anyone else to feel that way either.

She hurried down to the basement. One thing about The Armstrong, it was super organised. She checked the ledger book and quickly found where to look. Granted, the room she entered was a little cluttered and dusty. But it wasn't impossible to find all the cardboard boxes. The tree that once stood in the main entrance was twenty-five feet tall. How impressive it must have looked.

She found some more appropriate-sized decorations and put them into a box to carry upstairs.

Two hours later, just as the sky had darkened to shades of navy blue and purple, she'd finally achieved the effect she wanted.

Tiny white sparkly lights lit up a tree in the

corner of the main room. A gold star adorned the top. She'd found other multi-coloured twinkling lights that she'd wrapped around the curtain pole in the bedroom. She'd even strung a garland with red Christmas baubles above the bathroom mirror.

Each room had a little hint of Christmas. It wasn't overwhelming. But it was cute. It was welcoming. It gave the room the personal touch. The thoughtfulness that could occasionally be missing from even an exclusive hotel like this.

She walked around each room once again, taking in the mood she'd created. The Christmas style potpourri she'd found added to the room, filling it with the aroma of Christmas spices and adding even more atmosphere. She closed her eyes for a second and breathed in. She just loved it. She just loved everything about it.

Seeing the sky darkening with every second and snow dusting the streets outside, she gave a little smile.

Just one more touch.

She lifted the Christmas angel from the tissue paper and gently placed it on the pillow in the bedroom. She hadn't felt this good in a long time.

'Perfect,' she whispered.

'Just what do you think you're doing?' The voice poured ice all over her.

Finlay Armstrong was tired. He was beyond tired. He hadn't slept in three days. He'd ping-ponged between Japan, the USA and now the UK, all while fending off concerned phone calls from his parents. It was always the same at this time of year.

When would they realise that he deliberately made things busy at this time of year because it was the only way he could get through the season of goodwill?

He'd already ordered room service in his chauffeur-driven car on the journey from the airport. Hopefully it would arrive in the next few minutes then he could sleep for the next few hours and forget about everything.

He hadn't expected anyone to be in his penthouse. Least of all touching something that was so personal to him—so precious to him.

And the sight of it filled him with instant anger.

He hated Christmas. *Hated it.* Christmas cards with happy families. Mothers, fathers and their children with stockings hanging from the fireplace. The carols. The presents. The celebratory meals. All yearly reminders of what he had lost.

All reminders of another year without Anna.

The tiny angel was the one thing he had left. Her favourite Christmas decoration that she'd made as a child and used to hang from their tree every year with sentimental pride.

It was the one—and only—thing that had escaped the purge of Christmas for him.

And he couldn't even bear to look at it. He kept it tucked away and hidden. Just knowing it was there—hidden in the folds of his bag—gave him a tiny crumb of comfort that others clearly wouldn't understand.

But someone else touching it? Someone else unwrapping it? The only colour he could see right now was red.

Her head shot around and her eyes widened. She stepped backwards, stumbling and making a grab for the wall. 'Oh, I'm sorry. I was just trying to get the room ready for you.'

He frowned. He didn't recognise her. Didn't recognise her at all. Her shiny brown hair seemed to have escaped from the bun it was supposed to be in with loose strands all around her face.

There was an odd smear across one cheek. Was she dirty?

His eyes darted up and down the length of her body. An intruder in his room? No. She was definitely in uniform, but not quite *his* uniform. She had a black fitted shirt and skirt on, a white apron and black heeled shoes. There was a security key clipped to her waist.

'Who are you?' He stepped forward and pulled at her security badge, yanking it from the clip that held it in place. She let out a gasp and flattened against the wall, both hands up in front of her chest.

What? Did she think he might attack her in some way?

He waved the card. 'Who on earth are the Maids in Chelsea? Where are my regular housekeeping staff?'

She gave a shudder. *A shudder.* His lack of patience was building rapidly. The confused look on her face didn't help. Then things seemed to fall into place.

It was easy to forget how strong his Scottish accent could become when he was angry. It often took people a few seconds to adjust their ears to what he was saying.

'Maids in Chelsea is Clio Caldwell's company. I've worked for her for the last few months.' The words came out in a rush. She glanced around the room. 'I've been here for the last few months. Before that—I was in Knightsbridge. But I wasn't here.' She pointed to the floor. 'I've never been in here before.' She was babbling. He'd obviously made her nervous and that hadn't been his intention.

He pointed to the angel on the pillow. He could hardly even look at it right now. 'And is this what your work normally involves? Touching things you have no business touching? Prying into people's lives?' He looked around the room and shook his head. He couldn't help himself. He walked over to the curtains and gave the annoying flickering lights a yank, pulling them so sharply that they flickered once more then went out completely. 'Putting cheap, tacky Christmas decorations up in the rooms of The Armstrong?' The anger started to flare again. 'The Armstrong doesn't do this. We don't spread Christmas tat around as if this were some cheap shop. Where on earth did these come from?'

She looked momentarily stunned. 'Well?' he pressed.

She seemed to find her tongue again. 'They're not cheap. The box they were in said they cost five hundred pounds.' She looked at the single strand of lights he'd just broken and her face paled. 'I hope that doesn't come out of my wages.'

The thought seemed to straighten out her current confusion. She took a deep breath, narrowed her gaze at him and straightened her shoulders. She held up one hand. 'Who are *you*?'

Finlay was ready to go up like a firework. Now, he was being questioned in his own hotel, about who *he* was?

'I'm Finlay Armstrong. I'm the owner of The Armstrong and a whole host of other hotels across the world.' He was trying hard to keep his anger under control. He was tired. He knew he was tired. And he hadn't meant to frighten her. But whoever this woman was, she was annoying him. 'And I take it I'm the person that's paying your wages—though I'm not sure for how much longer.'

She tilted her chin towards him and stared him in the eye. 'I'd say it's a pleasure to meet you, Mr Armstrong, but we both know that wouldn't be true.'

He almost smiled. Almost. Her dark brown

eyes were deeper than any he'd seen before. He hadn't noticed them at first—probably because he hadn't been paying attention. But now he was getting the full effect.

He still wanted to have something to eat, crawl into bed, close the curtains and forget about the world outside. But this woman had just gained his full attention.

The tilt of her chin had a defiant edge to it. He liked that. And while her hair was a little unkempt and he still hadn't worked out what the mark was on her cheek, now those things were fading.

She was quite beautiful. Her hair must be long when it was down. Her fitted shirt showed off her curves and, although every part of her body was hidden, the white apron accentuated her slim waist and long legs.

She blinked and then spoke again. 'Clio doesn't take kindly to her staff being yelled at.'

'I didn't yell,' he replied instantly.

'Yes, you did,' she said firmly.

She bent down and picked up the broken strand of lights. 'I'm sorry you don't appreciate the Christmas decorations. They are all your own— of course. I got them from the basement.' She licked her lips for a second and then spoke again. 'I often think hotels can be a little impersonal. It can be lonely this time of year—particularly for those who are apart from their family. I was trying to give the room—' she held up her hands '—a little personality. That's all. A feeling of Christmas.' It was the wistful way she said it. She wasn't trying to be argumentative. He could tell from the expression on her face that she meant every word.

His stomach curled. The one thing he was absolutely trying to avoid. He didn't want to feel Christmas in any shape or form. He didn't want a room with 'feelings'. That was the whole point of being here.

He wanted The Armstrong to look sleek and exclusive. He'd purposely removed any sign of Christmas from this hotel. He didn't need reminders of the time of year.

For the first time in a long time he felt a tiny pang of regret. Not for himself, but for the person who was standing in front of him who clearly had demons of her own.

She pressed her lips together and started picking up the other decorations. She could move quickly when she wanted to. The red baubles were swept from above the bathroom mirror—he hadn't even noticed them yet. She stuffed the small tree awkwardly into the linen bag on her trolley. The bowl with—whatever it was—was tipped into the bin.

Her face was tight as she moved quickly around the penthouse removing every trace of Christmas from the room. As she picked up the last item—a tiny sprig of holly—she turned to face him.

'What is it you have against Christmas anyway?' She was annoyed. Upset even.

He didn't even think. 'My wife is dead and Christmas without her is unbearable.'

No one asked him that question. Ever. Not in the last five years.

Everyone tiptoed around about him. Speaking in whispers and never to his face. His friends had stopped inviting him to their weddings and christening celebrations. It wasn't a slight. It was their way of being thoughtful. He would never dream of attending on his own. And he just couldn't bear to see his friends living the life he should have with Anna.

The words just came spilling out unguarded. They'd been caught up inside him for the last five years. Simmering under the surface when people offered their condolences or gave that fleeting glance of pity.

'I hate Christmas. I hate everything about it. I hate seeing trees. I hate seeing presents. I hate seeing families all happy, smiling at each other. I don't need any reminders of the person missing from my life. I don't need any at all. I particularly don't need some stranger digging through my belongings and taking out the last thing I have of my wife's—the only thing that I've kept from our Christmases together—and laying it on my pillow like some holy talisman. Will it bring Anna back? Will it make Christmas any better?' He was pacing now. He couldn't help the pitch of his voice. He couldn't help the fact that the more he said, the louder he became, or the broader his Scottish accent sounded. 'No. No, it won't. So I don't do Christmas. I don't want to do it. And I don't want to discuss it.'

He turned back around to face her.

She looked shell-shocked. Her eyes wide and her bottom lip actually trembling. Her hand partially covering her mouth.

He froze. Catching himself before he continued any further.

There were a few seconds of silence. Tears

pooled in her eyes. 'I'm s…sorry,' she stammered as she turned on her heel and bolted to the door.

Finlay didn't move. Not a muscle. He hadn't even taken his thick winter coat off since he'd arrived.

What on earth had he just done?

He had no idea who the Maids in Chelsea were. He had no idea who Clio Caldwell was.

But he didn't doubt that as soon as she found him, he could expect a rollicking.

CHAPTER TWO

ONCE THE TEARS started she couldn't stop them. They were coming out in that weird, gasping way that made her feel as if she were fighting for every breath. She stopped in front of the elevator and fumbled for her card.

No! She didn't have it. He still did.

She looked around. Fire exit. It was the only other way out of here. There was no way she was hanging around.

As soon as she swung the door open she started upwards instead of down. Her chest was tight. She needed some air and she must be only seconds away from the roof. The grey door loomed in front of her. Was everything in this place black or grey? She pushed at the door and it sprang open onto the flat roof.

The rush of cold air was instant. She walked across the roof as she tried to suck some in.

She hadn't even thought about the cold. She hadn't even considered the fact it might still be snowing. The hotel was always warm so her thin shirt was no protection against the rapidly dipping temperatures on a late December afternoon.

But Grace couldn't think about the cold. All she could think about was the man she'd just met—Finlay Armstrong.

The expressions on his face. First of anger, then of disgust, a second of apparent amusement and then the soul-crushing, heart-ripped-out-of-his-chest look.

She'd done that to him. A stranger.

She'd caused him that amount of pain by just a few actions—just a few curious words.

She shivered involuntarily as the tears started to stream down her face. He'd implied that he'd sack her.

It was Christmas. She'd have no job. How could she afford to stay in the flat? As if this Christmas weren't already going to be hard enough without Gran, now she'd absolutely ruined whatever chance there was of having a peace-filled Christmas.

Her insides curled up and tumbled around. Why had she touched that angel? Why had she thought she had a right to decorate his room? And why, why had she blurted out that question?

The look on his face…the pain in those blue eyes. She shivered again. He'd lost his wife and because of that he couldn't bear Christmas. He didn't want to celebrate, didn't want to be reminded of anything.

The little things, the little touches she'd thought he might like, the tree, the decorations, the lights and the smells had all haunted him in a way she hadn't even imagined or even considered. What kind of a person did that make her?

She knew what it was like to find Christmas hard. A hundred little things had brought tears to her eyes this year—even while she was trying to ignore them. The smell of her gran's favourite perfume. The type of biscuit she'd most enjoyed at Christmas. Even the TV listing magazine where she used to circle everything she wanted to watch. But none of that—none of that—compared to the pain of a man who'd lost his wife.

Her gran had led a good and long life. His wife? She could only imagine how young she must have been. No wonder he was angry. No wonder he was upset.

She squeezed her eyes closed. She hadn't managed to find someone she'd made that special connection with yet. Someone she truly loved with her whole heart. Imagine finding them only to have them ripped away. How unfair must that feel?

The shivering was getting worse. Thick flakes of snow started to land on her face. She stared out across London. The views from the penthouse were already spectacular. But from the roof? They were something else entirely.

It was darker now and if she spun around she could see the whole of Chelsea spread out in front of her. The Armstrong's roof was the highest point around. The streets below looked like something from a Christmas card. Warm glowing yellow lights from the windows of the white Georgian houses, with roofs topped with snow. There were a few tiny figures moving below. People getting excited for Christmas.

The tears flowed harder. Battersea Power Station glowed in the distance. The four distinctive chimneys were usually lit up with white lights. But this time of year, the white lights were interspersed with red—to give a seasonal effect.

Every single bit of Christmas spirit she'd ever had had just disintegrated all around her.

Perfect Christmas. No job. No family. A mother

on the other side of the world who couldn't care less. And probably pneumonia.

Perfect.

The realisation hit him like a boxer's right hook.

What had he just done?

There was a roaring in his ears. He didn't behave like this. He would never behave like this. What on earth had possessed him?

All thoughts of eating, pulling the blinds and collapsing into bed vanished in an instant.

He rushed out into the hall. Where had she gone? Her chambermaid cart was abandoned in the hall. His eyes went to the panel above the elevator. But no, it wasn't moving. It was still on this floor.

Something cut into the palm of his hand. He looked down. The plastic identity card. Of course. He'd taken it from her. She couldn't use the elevator.

He strode back into his room and picked up the phone. He hadn't recognised the new receptionist. Officially—he hadn't even checked in.

The phone answered after one ring. 'What can I do for you, Mr Armstrong?'

'Frank? Who are the Maids in Chelsea?'

There was a second of silence. The question obviously caught the concierge unaware.

He could almost picture the way Frank sucked the air through his teeth when he was thinking—he could certainly hear it.

'Staff from the Maids in Chelsea company have been working here for the last four months, Mr Armstrong. There were some...issues with some of our chambermaids and Mr Speirs decided to take a recommendation from a fellow hotel.' Frank paused and then continued, 'We've had no problems. The girls are excellent. Mrs Archer, in particular, really loves Grace and asks for her whenever she's on duty.'

He cut right to the chase. 'What were the issues, Frank?'

The sucking sound echoed in his ear. He would have expected Rob Speirs to tell him of any major changes in the way his prestigious hotel was run. But Speirs was currently in hospital after an emergency appendectomy. That was part of the reason that he was here at short notice.

'There were some minor thefts. The turnover of staff was quite high. It was difficult to know where the problem lay.'

'And Rob—where did he get the recommendation?'

'From Ailsa Hillier. The Maids in Chelsea came highly recommended and we've had no problems at all.' There was another hesitation. 'Mr Armstrong, just to let you know, I have something for you.'

'What is it?'

'It's from Mrs Archer. She left something with me to pass on.'

Now he was curious. 'What is it, Frank?'

'It's a Christmas present.'

Frank was silent for a few seconds. Just as well really. Every hair on Finlay's body stood on end. Of course, he'd received Christmas presents over the last few years. His parents and sister always sent something. But Mrs Archer? This was a first.

Frank cleared his throat again. 'Mr Armstrong, is there anything I can help you with?'

This time it was Finlay that paused. He liked Frank. He'd always liked Frank. The guy knew everything that happened in his hotel—including the fact that his manager had used a company recommended by their rivals at the Corminster—interesting.

'Keep a hold of the present, I'll get it from you later, Frank.' It wouldn't be good to seem ungracious. Then he asked what he really wanted to know. 'Have you seen Grace Ellis in the last five minutes?'

'Grace? What's wrong with Grace?'

Finlay really didn't want to get into this. He could already hear the protectiveness in Frank's voice. He should have guessed it would be there. 'Nothing's wrong, but have you seen her?'

'No, sir. Not in the last hour at least.'

Finlay put down the phone. She could easily have run out but he had the strangest feeling that she hadn't.

He walked back outside, leaving the penthouse door open behind him and heading towards the stairs. When he pushed the door open he felt a rush of cold air around him.

The roof. She'd gone to the roof.

He ran up the stairs, two at a time, pausing when he reached the top.

She was standing at the end of the roof, staring out over London. She wasn't thinking of…

No. She couldn't be. But the fleeting thought made him reluctant to shout her back in.

He crossed the roof towards her. As he neared he could see she was shivering—shivering badly.

He reached out and touched her shoulder and she jumped.

'Grace? What are you doing out here? You'll freeze.'

She must have recognised his voice but she didn't turn towards him. Her arms were folded across her chest and more wisps of her hair had escaped from the bun.

He walked around slowly, until he was in front of her, blocking her view.

Her lips were tinged with blue and her face streaked with tears.

Guilt washed over him like a tidal wave.

Him. He'd caused this. He'd made this girl cry.

Why? After five years he'd thought he was just about ready to move on. But Christmas was always the hardest time for him. He was frustrated with the rest of the world for enjoying Christmas when it only brought back what he had lost.

Thank goodness he still had his coat on. He undid the buttons and shrugged it off, slipping it around her shoulders.

She still hadn't spoken to him. She was just looking at him with those huge brown eyes. The ones that had caught his attention in the first place. The ones that had sparked the reaction he should never have had.

Why was that? He'd always kept things locked inside. His friends knew that. They knew better than to try and discuss things. They spent their lives avoiding Anna's name or any of the shared memories they had of her.

'I'm sorry,' he said hoarsely. 'I should never have shouted at you.'

She blinked. Her eyes went down to her feet. 'I should never have decorated the room. I'm sorry,' she whispered.

He shook his head. 'No, Grace. You were trying to do something nice. Something sweet.' The words made his insides twist a little. Was it really so long that someone had done something sweet around him?

She blinked again. The shivering hadn't stopped yet and he could tell why. The wind was biting through his thin knit black jumper. It didn't matter he had a shirt underneath. It had been a long time since he'd felt this cold.

She bit her bottom lip. 'I... I sometimes forget that other people don't like Christmas. I should have been more sensitive. I should have thought things through.' A tear slid down her cheek. 'Did you come up here to fire me?'

'What? No.' He couldn't believe it. That was the last thing on his mind right now.

She looked confused. 'But you said…you said—'

'Forget what I said,' he cut in. 'I was being an idiot. I'm tired. I haven't slept in three days. I'm sorry—I know it's no excuse.'

'I'm sorry about your wife,' she whispered.

It came out of the blue. Entirely unexpected.

Sweeping through him like the brisk breeze of cold air around him.

It was the waver in her voice. He'd heard this a thousand times over the last few years. Most of the times the words had seemed meaningless. Automatically said by people who were sometimes sincere, sometimes not.

This woman—Grace—hadn't known his wife at all. But there was something about her—something he couldn't quite put his finger on. It was as if she knew mourning, she *knew* loss. It was probably the sincerest he'd ever heard those words spoken and it twigged a little part inside him.

He stepped back a little. He stepped back and sucked in a breath, letting the cold air sear the inside of his lungs. She was staring at him again. Something about this woman's vulnerable eyes did things to him.

He wanted to protect her. He wanted to make sure that no one hurt her. There was something else. It wasn't sympathy in her eyes.

He couldn't stand the look of sympathy. It only filled him with rage and self-loathing.

A tear slid down her cheek and the wave of protectiveness that was simmering beneath the surface washed over him completely.

He couldn't help himself. He reached up with his thumb and brushed it away, feeling the coolness of her smooth skin beneath the tip.

He stepped closer again. 'Don't,' he said quickly, his voice rising above a whisper. 'I'm sorry I made you feel like this.' He wanted to glance away—to have the safety of looking out over the capital's skyline—but Grace's chocolate gaze pulled him in. His hand was still at the side of her face. She hadn't pulled away. 'I meant what I said.' He pressed his lips together. 'Christmas brings out the worst in me. It just brings back too many memories. And I know... I know that not everyone feels like that. I know that maybe...just maybe I should be able to get past this.' A picture swam into his head and he let out a wry laugh. 'As for the Christmas decorations in the hotel? They might be a little on the sparse side.'

It was the oddest situation. The most bizarre he'd ever found himself in. The irony of it almost killed him. If someone had told him twenty-four hours ago that he'd end up on the roof of his hotel, in the snow, with a strange, enigmatic woman who was causing the shades to start to fall away from his eyes after five years, he would have laughed in their face.

He wasn't joking about the sparseness of the hotel. Rob Speirs had emailed to say some of the guests were complaining about the lack of Christmas spirit. Rob had also dropped a few hints that it was bad for business.

Grace's eyebrows arched. The edges of her lips turned upwards. 'You think?'

He put his arm around her shoulders. 'It's freezing out here—and only one of us has a coat. Let's go back inside.'

She hesitated for the tiniest second then gave a shiver and a nod as they started walking to the door. 'So you can fire me in comfort?'

'Less of the firing thing. Are you going to bring this up all the time?'

She nodded. 'Probably.'

He pulled open the door. 'How about we go downstairs for some hot chocolate and you can tell me more about Maids in Chelsea? I have it on good authority you've got a fan in Mrs Archer.'

Grace nodded. 'I thought you were tired. You said you hadn't slept in three days. You don't need to talk to me. We can just call it quits and I'll go home now.'

He shook his head as they stepped inside and walked down the stairs. 'Oh, no. You don't get off that easy. We have things to discuss.'

'We do?'

She sounded surprised. He swiped a key fob next to the elevator and the doors swished open. He gestured with his hand for her to go inside. 'You don't want to have hot chocolate with me?'

He made it sound light-hearted. He wanted to try and make amends for his earlier behaviour. But the truth was his curiosity was piqued by Grace.

She gave him a cheeky stare. 'Only if there are marshmallows and cream. I get the impression you might be a bit of a cheapskate.'

He laughed as she walked into the elevator and for the first time in five years something happened.

It had been so long he almost didn't recognise it.

His heart gave a little leap.

Grace wasn't quite sure what to make of any of this. One minute Mr Film Star looks was firing her in his gravelly Scottish voice, the next minute he was apologising and making her heart completely stop when he touched her cheek.

It was the weirdest feeling. She'd been beyond cold—but the touch of his finger on her cheek had been like a little flame sending pulses around her body.

They stood in silence as the elevator moved silently to the ground floor. Frank caught sight of them as they walked out into the foyer, but Finlay didn't give them time to talk. He ushered her through to one of the private sitting rooms, speaking to a waitress on the way past.

They sat down on the comfortable black velvet-covered chairs. She ran her hand over the material. 'Black. Nice,' she said as she watched his face.

He shook his head. 'I feel that you might be going to make me pay.'

The strange wariness she'd felt around him had seemed to vanish. She'd seen something up on that roof. Something she'd never seen in another person.

For a few moments it had felt as if she could see right into his soul. His pain. His hurt. His bitterness.

He seemed to be at a point in his life that she couldn't even begin to understand.

'Me? Make you pay? Whatever makes you think that?'

He put one elbow on the table and leaned on his hand. He did still look tired, but there was a little sparkle in those blue eyes. When Finlay Armstrong wasn't being so businesslike and generally miserable, he showed tiny glimmers of a sense of humour.

The good looks were still there. Now she wasn't so flabbergasted she could see them clearly. In fact, in the bright lights of the hotel his handsome features might even be a bit intimidating.

But there was something about that accent—that Scottish burr—that added something else to the mix. When she'd first heard it—that fierceness—its tone of *don't ever cross me* had had her shaking in her shoes. Now, there was a softness. A warmth about the tone.

He held out his arms to the room they were sitting in. 'I chose black and grey deliberately. I liked the smoothness, sleekness and no-nonsense look of the hotel. White would have been clinical. Any other colour just a distraction that would age quickly. Black and grey are pretty timeless colours.'

'If you can call them colours.'

The waitress appeared and set down steaming hot chocolates, adorned with marshmallows and cream, and long spoons. The aroma drifted up instantly. After the coldness of outside the instant warmth was comforting.

Finlay spooned some of the cream from his hot chocolate into his mouth and gave a loud sigh. 'I'm guessing you don't like my interior design selections.'

Grace smiled and tried to catch some of her marshmallows before they melted. 'I bet they cost more money than I could earn in ten years.'

He stopped stirring his hot chocolate and looked at her.

She cringed. Did she really mean to say that out loud?

The marshmallows-and-cream assortment was all sticking together inside her mouth. Any minute now she would start choking. She took another quick sip of the hot chocolate in an attempt to melt some of the marshmallows before she needed emergency treatment. Seemed as if she'd brought enough attention to herself already.

'How would you like to earn some more money?'

Too late. She coughed and spluttered everywhere. Did he really just say *that*?

As quickly as the words left his mouth and Grace started choking, Finlay Armstrong started to laugh.

He did. The guy actually started laughing. He leaned over and started giving her back a few slaps, trying to stop her choking. He was shaking his head. 'I didn't mean that. I didn't mean anything like that. It's okay, Grace. You don't need to fake a medical emergency and escape in an ambulance.'

The choking started to subside and Finlay signalled over to one of the waitresses to bring some water. He was still laughing.

Her cheeks were warm. No, her cheeks were red hot. Between choking to death and thinking completely inappropriate thoughts she couldn't be any more embarrassed if she tried.

Because she had thought inappropriate thoughts—even if it had been for just a millisecond.

She hadn't had enough time to figure out if she was mortally offended and insulted, or just completely and utterly stunned.

A bartender in a sleek black dress came over with a bottle of water and some glasses with ice. She shot Finlay her best sultry smile as she poured the water for them both. Grace got a look of disdain. Perfect.

The water-pouring seemed to take for ever. She could almost hear some sultry backtrack playing behind them.

Finlay was polite but reserved. The bartender got the briefest of thanks, then he turned his attention back to Grace. It was hard not to grab the glass and gulp the water down. She waited until the water was finally poured, then gave her most equally polite smile and took some eager sips.

She cleared her throat. 'I didn't think that, you know,' she said quickly.

Finlay laughed even harder than before. 'Yes.' He nodded. 'You did. My bad. The wrong choice of words. I didn't mean that at all.'

She gulped again. Now they were out in public his conduct seemed a little different. He was laughing but there was more of a formality about him. This was his hotel and right now he was under the microscopic view of all his staff. He had a reputation to uphold. She got that. She did.

And right now his eyes didn't show any hint of the vulnerability she'd glimpsed upstairs. Now, his eyes seemed like those of a worldly-wise businessman. One that had probably seen and done things she could only ever dream of.

All she knew about Finlay Armstrong was the little he'd told her. But Finlay had the self-assured aura that lots of self-made businessmen had.

The knowledge, the experience, the know-how and the confidence that a lot of the clients she'd met through Maids in Chelsea had. People who had lived entirely different lives from the one she had.

She set down her water and tried to compose herself again. Heat had finally started to permeate into her body. She could feel her fingers and toes.

She finally shook off Finlay's coat. She'd forgotten it was around her shoulders. That was what the bartender had been staring at.

She tugged at her black shirt, straightening it a little, and put her hand up to her hair, trying to push it back into place.

Finlay was watching her with amusement. 'Leave it—it's fine. Let's talk about something else.'

Grace shifted a little on the velvet chair. What on earth did he want to talk to her about?

His hands ran up and down the outside of the latte glass. 'I'd like you to take on another role within the hotel.'

She sat up a bit more. Her curiosity was definitely piqued. 'What do you mean?'

He held out his hands around the room. 'You mentioned the lack of Christmas decorations and I think you might be right. Rob Speirs, my manager, mentioned there's been a few complaints. He thinks it could be affecting business. It might be time to have a rethink.'

She tilted her head to the side. 'You want me to bring up the stuff from the basement?'

He shook his head. 'No. I don't want any of the old decorations. I want new. I want you to look around and think of a theme for the hotel, something that gives the Christmas message while keeping the upmarket look that I like for the hotel.'

Grace's mouth fell open. 'What?'

He started a little. 'And obviously I'll pay you. A designer fee, plus a company credit card to cover all the costs and delivery of what you choose.'

Grace was having trouble believing this. He'd pulled the few decorations she'd put up in the penthouse down with his bare hands. He'd called them tacky. Now, he wanted her to decorate the whole hotel?

She couldn't help the nervous laugh that sneaked out. 'Finlay, do you know what date it is?'

He wrinkled his nose. 'The sixteenth? The seventeenth of December? Sorry, I've crossed so many time zones lately I can't keep track.'

She shook her head. 'I don't know for sure, but I'm guessing most of the other hotels decided on their Christmas schemes months ago—and ordered all their decorations. They've had their decorations up since the middle of November.'

Finlay shook his head. 'That's too early. Even the first day of December seems too soon.'

Grace leaned across the table towards him. 'I'm not sure that what you have in mind and what I have in mind will be the same thing.'

'What do you mean?'

She sighed and tried to find appropriate words. 'Less than half an hour ago you told me you hated Christmas and everything about it. What's changed your mind?'

The hesitation was written all over his face. Just as she'd done a few seconds earlier, he was trying to find the right words. She could almost see them forming on his lips. She held her breath. Then, just when he looked as if he might answer, he leaned forward and put his head in his hands.

Now she definitely couldn't breathe. She pressed her lips together to stop herself from filling the silence.

When Finlay looked up again, it wasn't the polished businessman she'd been sitting opposite for the last twenty minutes. This was Finlay, the guy on the roof who'd lost his wife and seemed to lose himself in the process. What little oxygen supplies she had left sucked themselves out into the atmosphere in a sharp burst at the unhidden pain in his eyes.

'It's time.' His voice cracked a little and his

shoulders sagged as if the weight that had been pressing him down had just done its last, awful deed.

She couldn't help herself. She didn't care about appropriateness. She didn't care about talk. Grace had always had a big heart. She always acted on instinct. She slid her hand across the glass-topped table and put it over his.

It didn't matter that the word no had been forming on her lips. It didn't matter that she felt completely out of her depth and had no qualifications for the position he wanted to give her. She squeezed his hand and looked him straight in the eye, praying that her tears wouldn't pool again.

He gave himself a shake and straightened up. 'And it's a business decision.' He pulled his hand back.

She gave him a cautious smile. 'If you're sure— and it's a business decision,' she threw in, even though she didn't believe it, 'the answer is yes.'

He leaned back against the chair, his shoulders straightening a little.

'I have to warn you,' she continued, 'that the picture you see in your head might not match the picture I have in mine.'

She glanced across the room and gave him a

bigger smile. 'I can absolutely promise you that no matter how sleek, no matter how modern you think they are—there will be no black Christmas trees in The Armstrong hotel.'

The shadows fell a little from his eyes. 'There won't?'

There was the hint of a teasing tone in his voice. As if he was trying his best to push himself back from the place he'd found himself in.

'My Christmas could never have black trees. I'll do my best to keep things in the style you like. But think of Christmas as a colour burst. A rainbow shower.' She held up one hand as she tried to imagine what she could do. 'A little sparkle on a gloomy day.'

Finlay nodded in agreement. . 'I'll get you a credit card. Is there anything else you need?'

She licked her lips. Her throat was feeling dry. What had she just got herself into?

Her brain started to whizz. 'Use of a phone. And a computer. A space in one of the offices if you can.'

Finlay stood up. 'I can do that.'

It seemed the businessman persona had slotted back into place. Then, there was a tiny flicker of something behind his eyes.

He smiled and held out his hand towards her. She stood up nervously and shook his hand. 'Grace Ellis, welcome to The Armstrong Hotel.'

CHAPTER THREE

'WHAT'S WRONG WITH you today?' asked Alice.

Grace was staring out of the window, lack of sleep making her woozy.

She turned her attention back to Alice. 'Nothing, I'm sorry. I'm just a little tired.'

Alice narrowed her gaze with a sly smile on her face. 'I've seen that kind of distracted look before—just not on you.'

Grace finished making the bed and turned to face Alice. 'I don't know what you mean.'

The last thing she wanted to do was admit to Alice the reasons that sleep had evaded her. It would be easy to say it was excitement about the job offer. Stress about whether she could actually *do* the job. But the truth was—while they might have contributed—the main sleep stealer had been the face that kept invading her mind every few seconds.

There was something so enigmatic about Finlay Armstrong. It wasn't just the traditional good looks, blue eyes and sexy Scottish accent. It was something so much more.

And there was no way she could be the only one that felt it.

A successful businessman like Finlay Armstrong must have women the world over trying to put themselves on his radar.

She had no idea how he behaved in private. Five years was a long time. Had he had any hook ups since his wife died? Probably. Surely?

She didn't even want to think like that.

It was just…that moment…that moment on the roof. The expression in his eyes. The way he'd looked at her when he'd reached up and touched her cheek.

Grace hadn't wanted to acknowledge how low she'd been feeling up there. She hadn't wanted to admit how she was missing her gran so much it felt like a physical pain.

But for a few seconds—up on that roof—she'd actually thought about something else.

She'd actually only thought about Finlay Armstrong.

'Grace?' Alice Archer had walked over and touched her arm.

'Oh, sorry, Alice. I was miles away.'

Alice raised her eyebrows. 'And where was that exactly?'

Grace bit her lip and pulled some folded papers from her white apron. 'I've to help choose some Christmas decorations for the hotel. I was up half the night trying to find something appropriate.'

Alice gave a little smile and reached her thin hand over to look at the printouts. Grace swallowed. She could see the blue veins under Alice's pale skin. A few of her knuckle joints were a little gnarled. They must give her pain—but she never complained. Another reminder of how much she missed her gran.

Alice glanced over the pictures, her eyes widening at a few. Grace had spent hours tracking down themes and stockists for particular items. All of them at costs that made her blink.

Alice gave her a thoughtful look as she handed the pictures back. She patted Grace's hand. 'I'm sure whatever you choose will be perfect. It will be nice to have some Christmas cheer around the hotel.'

Grace couldn't help but smile. 'Christmas cheer, that's exactly what I'm trying to capture. Something to make people get in the spirit.'

Alice walked over to her Louis XV velvet-covered chair and sank down with a wince.

'Are you okay? Are you hurting?'

Alice shook her head proudly and folded her hands in her lap. 'No. I'm not sore, Grace. I'm just old. I'll have some lemon tea now, if you please.'

'Of course.' Grace hurried over to complete their morning ritual. She sliced the fresh lemon and prepared the tea, boiling the water and carrying the tray with the china teapot and cup and saucer over to the table at Alice's elbow.

Alice gave a grateful sigh. Her make-up was still impeccable but her eyes were tired this morning. 'Maybe you should have some help? Someone to give you some confidence in your decisions.'

Grace was surprised. 'Do you want to come with me? You're more than welcome to. I would be glad of the company.'

Alice laughed and shook her head. 'Oh, no. I don't mean me. I was thinking more of someone else…someone else who could use a little Christmas spirit.'

Grace had poured the tea and was about to hand the cup and saucer to Alice but her hand wobbled. She knew exactly who Alice was hinting about.

'I don't think that would be appropriate. He's far too busy. He's far too immersed in his work. He wouldn't have time for anything like that.'

She shifted uncomfortably. She had a pink shirt hanging up in her locker, ready to change into once she'd finished her chambermaid duties. Alice was staring at her with those steady grey eyes. It could be a little unnerving. It was as if she could see into Grace's head and see all the secret weird thoughts she'd been having about Finlay Armstrong since last night.

Gran had been a bit like that too. She'd always seemed to know what Grace was going to say before she even said it. Even when she'd been twelve years old and her friend had stolen a box of chocolates from the local shop. The associated guilt had nearly made Grace sick, and she'd only been home and under Gran's careful gaze for ten minutes before she'd spilled everything.

Alice Archer was currently sparking off a whole host of similar feelings.

Her eyes took on a straight-to-the-point look. 'He asked you to get him some Christmas decorations, didn't he?'

Grace set the cup and saucer down. 'Yes,' she replied hesitantly.

'Then, he's reached the stage that he's ready to start living again.'

The words were so matter-of-fact. So to the point. But Alice wasn't finished.

'It's time to bring a little Christmas magic to The Armstrong, Grace, and you look like just the girl to do it.'

One hour later the black shirt was crumpled in a bag and her long-sleeved deep pink shirt with funny little tie thing at the collar was firmly in place. She grabbed some more deodorant from her locker. She was feeling strangely nervous. A quick glance in the mirror showed her hair was falling out of its bun again. She pulled the clip from her hair and gave it a shake. Her hair tumbled in natural waves. She was lucky. It rarely needed styling. Should she redo her lipstick?

She pulled her plum lipstick from her bag and slicked some on her lips. There. She was done. She took a deep breath, reaching into the apron that she'd pushed into her locker for her array of pictures. Her last touch was the black suit jacket—the only one she owned. She'd used it for her interview with Clio some months ago and thought of it as her good luck charm.

Finally she was satisfied with how she looked. She'd never be wearing designer clothes, but she felt presentable for the role she was about to undertake.

She pushed everything else back into the locker and did her final job—swapping her square-heeled black shoes for some black stilettos. She teetered for the tiniest second and laughed. Who was she trying to kid? She pulled open the locker again and slid her hand into the inside pocket of her black bag. There. Drop gold earrings that her gran had given her for her twenty-first birthday. She usually only wore them on special occasions but in the last few months, and particularly at this time of year, she missed her gran more than she could ever say. She slipped them into her ears and straightened her shoulders, taking a deep breath.

There it was. The little shot of confidence that she needed. She glanced down at the papers in her hand and smiled.

She was going to give this hotel the spirit of Christmas no matter what.

* * *

He could hear a strange noise outside his room. Like a shuffling. After more than a few seconds it was annoying.

Finlay's first reaction was to shout. But something stopped him. Maybe it was Alice Archer? Could she have come looking for him?

He sat his pen down on his desk. 'Is someone there?'

The noise that followed was almost a squeak. He smiled and shook his head. 'Well, it's obviously an infestation of mice. I'd better phone the exterminator.'

'What? No!' Grace's head popped around the door.

Grace. It was funny the odd effect that had on him.

She kind of sidled into the office. 'I'm sorry if I'm disturbing you, Mr Armstrong.'

He gestured towards the chair in front of him. 'It's Finlay. If you call me Mr Armstrong I'll start looking over my shoulder for my father.'

She shot him a nervous smile and walked hesitantly across the room towards the chair.

He tried his best not to stare.

Grace had already caught his attention. But

now, she wasn't wearing the maid's outfit. Now, she had on a black suit and stiletto heels.

Finlay Armstrong had met a million women in black suits and heels. But he'd never met one quite like Grace. She had on a pink shirt with a funny tie at the neck.

And it was the colour that made him suck in his breath. It wasn't pale or bright, it was somewhere in the middle, a warm rose colour that brought out the colour in her cheeks and highlighted the tone of her lipstick. It suited her more than she could ever know.

Her hair swung as she walked across the room. It was the first time he'd seen it down. Okay, so the not staring wasn't going to work. Those chestnut curls were bouncing and shining like the latest shampoo TV advert.

Grace sat down in the chair opposite him fixing him with her warm brown eyes. She slid something across the desk towards him.

'I just wanted to check with you.' She licked her pink lips for a second. 'How, exactly, do I use this?'

He stared down at the company credit card. 'What do you mean?'

She bit her lip now and crossed one leg over

the other. Her skirt slid up her thigh and he tore his eyes away and fixed on her eyes.

Big mistake.

'I mean, do I sign—can I sign? Or do I need a pin number or something?'

'You haven't used a company credit card before?' He hadn't even considered it.

She shook her head. He could see the slight tremble to her body. She was nervous. She was nervous coming in here and asking him about this.

'Sorry, Grace. I should have left you some instructions.' He'd just left the card for her in an envelope at Reception. He scribbled down some notes. 'This is what you do.'

She leaned forward on the desk as he wrote and a little waft of her perfume drifted towards him. He'd smelled this before. When he'd been inches from her in the penthouse he'd inhaled sharply and caught this same scent, something slightly spicy with a little tang of fruit. He couldn't quite place which one it was.

He finished writing and looked up. 'Have you had some ideas about what you need for the hotel?'

She nodded and lifted up some papers in her

hand, unfolding them and sitting them on the desk. She still looked nervous. 'I know quality is important to you. But, because you've left things so late this year, I can't really pre-order or negotiate with anyone for a good price. We'll have to buy straight from the retailer. So...' she pressed her lips together for a second '...I've prepared three price ranges for you. You can let me know which one you prefer and we'll go with that one.'

He waved his hand. 'The price isn't important to me, Grace. The quality is.'

Her face fell a little. Wasn't that the right answer he'd just given her—that she had no limits to her spending? Any other designer he'd ever met would have cartwheeled out of the room at this point.

She shuffled her papers.

'What is it?'

She shook her head. 'Nothing.'

There were a hundred other things he could be doing right now. But since he had worked on the plane on the way home most things were up to date. Just as well really. After his experience last night, sleep hadn't come quite as easily as he'd expected.

Oh, he'd eventually blacked out. But he'd still managed to spend a few hours tossing and turning.

Her brown eyes were now fixed on those darn papers she was shuffling in her hands and he was strangely annoyed. He reached over and grabbed them.

It didn't take long to realise what he was looking at. He started to count them. 'Nine, ten, eleven, twelve... Grace, how many versions of these did you do?'

'Well, the first one was my absolute wish list. Then, I thought maybe you wouldn't want lights, or the big tree, or some of the other ideas I had, so I made a few other versions.'

He couldn't believe it. He'd only sprung this on her yesterday. The last company he'd worked with had taken three months just to give him a *quote* for something.

He shook his head. 'How long did this take you?'

She met his gaze again. It was clear she didn't really want to answer.

'Grace?'

She pulled a face. 'Maybe most of last night.'

'Until when, exactly?'

She pulled on her game face. 'I'm not sure exactly.'

He smiled and stood up, walking around towards her. She knew exactly how long it had taken her. He guessed she'd hardly had any sleep last night.

He put one leg on the desk, sitting just a few inches away from her. 'Grace, if I gave you free rein today, where would you go and what would you buy?'

She was silent for a few seconds. Then, her head gave a little nod. To his surprise she stood up.

Because he'd changed position she was only inches from his face. From close up, he had a much better view of her curves under her suit. He could see the upward and downward movements of her chest beneath the muted satin of her shirt.

Even more noticeable was her flawless complexion. There was a warmth about Grace. It seemed to emanate from her pores. Something trustworthy. But something else, a hint of vulnerability that just didn't seem to go away.

He'd seen other little glimpses. A spark of fire when he'd obviously annoyed her in the penthouse. She'd taken a deep breath and answered him back. Grace didn't like people treating her like a fool. She knew how to stand up for herself.

His smartphone buzzed and he glanced at it. An email he should deal with. But the truth was he didn't want to.

'What's your idea for the hotel?' he asked Grace.

She blinked at the suddenness of his question, but she didn't miss a beat. She held out her hands. 'I'm going to bring Christmas to The Armstrong. The hotel is missing something. Even you know that.' She raised her eyebrows. 'And you've given me the job of finding it.'

He picked up the phone on his desk and stared at her. 'Tell me where you're going and I'll order a car for you.'

She waved her hand and shook her head. 'I can catch the Tube.'

This time it was him that raised his eyebrows. 'Aren't you going to have some purchases to bring back?'

She put her hand up to her mouth. 'Oops.'

He asked again. 'So, where do you want the car to go?'

'First Selfridges, then Harrods, then Fortnum and Mason..' She didn't hesitate.

'You really think you can do all that in one day?'

She shook her head. 'Oh, no. I can do all that in an *afternoon*. You've obviously never met a professional Christmas shopper, Finlay.'

It was the first time she'd said his name. Actually said his name. And it was the way she said it. The way it rolled from her tongue with her London accent.

He spoke quickly into the phone on his desk, put it down and folded his arms across his chest. He smiled as he shook his head. 'No, I don't think I have.'

She wrinkled her brow. 'How old are you, exactly?' She matched his stance and stood in front of him with her arms folded across her chest.

It was almost like a challenge.

He stood up to his full height and stepped a tiny bit closer. He could take this challenge. 'Thirty-six.'

'Oh, dear.' She took a step backwards and put her hand up to her head. She looked out from under her hand with a wicked glint in her eye. 'Did you play with real live dinosaurs as a boy?' Her smile broadened as she continued. 'And shouldn't we watch the time? I guess you make all dinner reservations for around four-thirty p.m.—that's when all the early bird specials are, aren't they?'

He'd met a lot of people in this life—both before and after Anna—but he'd never met anyone who had the same effect as Grace. Even though she was officially an employee, he kept seeing glimpses of the woman underneath the uniform. Whether it was fun and jokes, a little melancholy or just a hint of real.

That was what it was.

Grace felt real. She was the only person who didn't seem to be watching how they acted around him—watching what they said. He liked the fact she was teasing him. Liked the fact she didn't treat him as if he were surrounded by broken glass.

'Seriously?'

She nodded. 'Seriously.' But it was clear she was teasing.

He laughed and shook his head and countered. 'You're probably not that much younger than me. You've just found some really good face cream.'

He handed over the company credit card as his phone rang. 'On you go and have some fun buying up any Christmas decorations that are left.' He answered the phone and put his hand over the

receiver. 'I look forward to seeing what a professional Christmas shopper can do.'

Sixty minutes later Finlay Armstrong didn't look
happy at all. He looked as if he were about to
erupt.

Grace cringed as he strode across the store towards her. She was already feeling a little in-
timidated. Three security guards were standing
next to her. She'd understandably almost been
out on the street. That was what happened when
you couldn't remember the pin number for
the credit card you were using or answer any
of the security questions.

Finlay walked over to the counter. 'What's the
problem?'

Once she started talking she couldn't stop.
She'd been having the time of her life. 'I've
bought a huge Christmas tree for the foyer of the
hotel, along with another two large trees for the
bar and the restaurant.' Then she held her hand up
towards the counter and the serious-faced woman
behind it. 'Well, I haven't really bought them. I
got here and...'

She held up the piece of paper that he'd given
her. It had managed to get smudged and the num-

bers on it were indecipherable. She leaned forward. 'Please tell them I really do work for the hotel. I'm not on their list and don't know any of the questions they asked me.'

Finlay's jaw tightened, but he turned and addressed the woman with impeccable politeness. 'I'm Finlay Armstrong. I own the company. I can either use the correct pin, or answer any of the security questions you need.'

The woman gave a nod. 'I'm afraid you'll have to do both on this occasion. And, Mr Armstrong, if you add another member of staff onto the card—you really should let us know.'

Grace wanted to sink through the floor. This shopping trip definitely wasn't going to plan. She was behind already.

Finlay was finished a few minutes later. 'If I give you the number, do you think you can remember it again?'

The staff member cleared her throat behind them, 'Actually, Mr Armstrong, your card has already been flagged today. You might be asked security questions if you use it again.'

Grace gulped. 'What does that mean?'

Finlay glanced at his watch. 'How much longer will this take?'

Grace glanced down at the list still in her hands. She wanted to lie and say around five minutes. But London traffic would be starting to get heavy. 'Probably another couple of hours.'

Finlay rolled his eyes. He stared off into the distance for a second. 'We need the decorations for the hotel,' he muttered. 'Okay, let's go. The car's outside.'

The cold air hit her as soon as they came outside and she shivered. 'Where's your coat?' he asked.

She shrugged. 'I just got so excited when you gave me the card and told me there was a car outside, I forgot to go and get my coat and gloves.' She shook her head. 'It doesn't really matter. We'll be inside for most of the time.'

The car pulled up and he held the door as she slid inside and he climbed in next to her. He was talking on the phone—obviously still doing business.

It wasn't deliberate. But all her senses seemed on alert. The wool from his black coat had brushed against her hand sending weird vibes everywhere. The aroma of his aftershave was slowly but surely drifting towards her in the warm atmosphere of the car. And even though it was cold outside, she was praying her pink shirt wouldn't show any unexpected perspiration marks.

It was only early afternoon but the sky already had a dark purple tinge at its edges.

Finlay glanced at his watch. There was a tiny shadow around his jaw line. The hint of a little stubble. Mixed with those unusual blue eyes it was enough to make any warm-blooded female catch her breath.

Part of her heart was going pitter-patter. So many expectations. What if he hated her ideas? What if he couldn't see how they translated to The Armstrong?

He closed his phone and leaned forward to speak to the driver. 'How much longer?'

'Just another ten minutes,' was the reply.

Grace felt nervous. Jumpy around him. Small talk seemed like the best solution.

'You mentioned your mum and dad earlier— are you spending time with them this year?'

He frowned. She wondered if he wasn't going to answer, then he shook his head. 'No. My parents are still in Scotland. My sister is expecting their first grandchild and will probably be fussed over non-stop.'

The answer was brisk. It was clear Christmas was still an issue for him—even if he was agreeing to decorations for the hotel.

As she went to speak again, her hand brushed against his. He flinched and then grabbed it. 'Grace, your hands are freezing.' He started rubbing his hands over hers. She was taken aback. After the frown it was a friendlier gesture than she might have expected.

His warming actions brought the aroma of the rose and lavender hand cream she'd used earlier drifting up between them. She hadn't even thought about how cold her hands were.

The car pulled up outside one of London's oldest and most distinguished department stores, Fortnum and Mason. Grace was so excited she didn't wait for the driver to come around and open the door—she was out in a flash. She waved at Finlay. 'Come on, slowcoach. Let's get started. We need Christmas wreaths and garlands.'

She walked swiftly, darting her way between displays and heading for the elevators. But Finlay's footsteps faltered. It was like...*whoosh*!

Christmas everywhere. Every display. Every member of staff. Perpetual Christmas tunes piping overhead. Grace had even started singing along. Did she even notice?

It was like Christmas overload.

It was clear he'd unleashed the monster. He hadn't seen someone this enthusiastic about Christmas since his sister was five years old and thought she might get a horse. She did—but it was around twelve inches.

He pushed back the wave of emotions that was in danger of rearing its ugly head. He'd chosen to be here. He'd decided it was time to try and move forward. The perpetual little ache he felt would always be there. But should it really last for ever?

They walked through the tea hall that was jostling with people. 'I love the Christmas shop in here. There's so much to choose from.' She kept talking as they darted between shoppers.

The lifts were small and lined with wood. He found himself face to face with her, their noses inches away from each other. In this confined space he felt instantly protective, his hand reaching up and resting on her hip.

She smiled and tipped her head to one side. 'Did you listen to a single word I said?'

He shook his head as the doors closed and the

piped music continued. 'Not a single word,' he admitted.

She gently slapped his chest. 'Shocker. Well, remember only these words: *I will not complain about the price.*'

He rolled his eyes. 'Grace, what are we buying in here?'

She still looked happy. It was obvious Christmas decorations were something that she just loved. 'I told you. Christmas wreaths and garlands to decorate the foyer, the bar, the corridors, the restaurant and the elevators.' She counted them off on her fingers.

He blinked for a second. Wreaths. He'd forgotten how often they were used as Christmas decorations now. It was almost as if the world had misplaced what they actually were.

They were lucky: no one else rode to the top floor with them. The elevator pinged and she looked over her shoulder. 'This is us.' She wiggled around, her backside pressing straight into him.

Finlay felt numb. No matter how she'd joked, he was still a young guy. And like any young man, his body reacted to a woman being up close and personal—even if it was unintentional.

Grace seemed not to have noticed anything. She dodged her way through the bodies.

As soon as they stepped outside the lift Grace almost started skipping. She handed him a basket and picked up a few delicate glass and white tree decorations. Then, she walked over to the counter. 'I phoned earlier about a special order. Wreaths and garlands—you said you'd put them aside for me.'

The clerk nodded. 'They're through here. Do you want to see them before you pay?'

Finlay let Grace work her magic. She was loving this. This wasn't the vulnerable woman that he'd seen on the rooftop. This was in control and in her element Grace. Within a few minutes he'd handed over the company credit card and heard her arrange for delivery in a few hours' time.

Grace let out a squeal. 'My favourite ever Christmas song—"Last Christmas"—let's sing along.'

He looked at her in surprise. 'This is your favourite song? It's not exactly cheery, is it?'

But Grace was oblivious and already singing along. A few fellow shoppers gave him an amused stare. She really was singing and didn't seem to care who was listening. The fleeting sad thoughts disappeared from his head again. Grace had a little glance at her lists and made a few random ticks before folding them up again and belting out the main part of the song.

The pink flush in her cheeks suited her. But what caught his attention most was the sparkle in those dark brown eyes. He wouldn't have thought it possible. But it was. He sucked in a breath. If he didn't watch out Grace Ellis could become infectious.

Grace came back and pressed her hand on his arm. 'I've seen a few other things I like. You stay here or it'll spoil the fun.' She waved her hand. 'Have a look around. I'll only be five minutes.'

He frowned as she disappeared. Fun?

He wandered around, watching people gaze in wonder at all the decorations. The garlands in store were beautiful. They had a whole range of colours and they covered walls, shelves and the Christmas fireplaces that had been set up in store. Next to them was a whole range of wreaths: some holly, some twisted white twigs, some traditionally green decorated with a variety of colours. He stopped walking.

He was looking at wreaths and not automatically associating them with Anna. Guilt washed over him. Shouldn't she always be his first thought?

But she hadn't been. Not for the last few months. It was as if his head was finally lifting from the fog it had been in these last five years. But Christmas time was a little different. It seemed to whip up more memories than usual. It made the thought of moving on just a little more tricky.

A little girl walked into him as she stared at a rocking horse. He bent down to speak to her. She was like something from a chocolate box. A red double-breasted wool coat, a little worn but clearly loved, dark curls poking out from under a black hat. She hadn't even realised she'd walked into him—her eyes were still on the white rocking horse with a long mane decorated with red saddle. She let out a little sigh.

'Come along, Molly,' said a harassed voice. 'We just came here for a little look. It's time to go.'

He lifted his head instantly. The woman looked tired—her clothes even more so. Her boots were worn, her jacket was missing a few buttons and the scarf she had wrapped around her neck looked almost as old as she was. But it was her accent that drew his attention.

He straightened up and held out his hand. 'Hi, Finlay Armstrong. What part of Scotland are you from?'

She was startled by his question and took a few seconds to answer. He could almost see the recognition of his own accent before she finally reached over and shook his hand. 'Hi, I'm Karen. I'm from Ayrshire.'

There was something in the wistful way she said it that made him realise this wasn't a visit.

He kept hold of her hand. 'Have you been in London long?'

She sighed. 'Three years. I had to move for work.'

He nodded his head towards the rocking horse. 'Your little girl was admiring the rocking horse.'

Karen winced. 'I know. I asked for one every year too as a child.' She glanced down at her child again then met his gaze. 'But we can all dream.'

He sucked in a breath. When was the last time he'd done something good? He'd been so wrapped in his own mourning for the last five years he hadn't really stopped to draw breath. Even when it came to Christmas presents he normally gave his PA a list and told her what kind of things his family preferred. That was as much input as he'd had.

He thought about the prettily wrapped present that Mrs Archer had left for him at reception. He hadn't even opened it yet.

He kept his voice low. 'How about Molly gets what she wants for Christmas?'

Karen looked shocked, then offended. He knew exactly how this worked. He shook his head. 'I work for a big company. Every year they like us to do a few good deeds. A few things that no one else finds out about.' He pulled the card out of his pocket, still keeping his voice low. 'There's no catch. I promise. Give the girl at the desk an address and time for delivery. That's all.'

Karen sucked in a breath. 'I don't want to be someone's good deed.' He could see her bristle.

He gave a nod of acknowledgement. 'Then how about a gift from a fellow Scot who is also missing home?'

Her eyes filled with tears and she put her hand to her throat. 'Oh…oh, then that might be different.'

He glanced down at Molly and smiled. 'Good. Just give the girl at the desk your details. I'll arrange everything else.'

'I don't know what to say, except thank you. And Merry Christmas!'

He gave her a nod. 'Happy Christmas to you and Molly.'

He ruffled Molly's curls and walked away, not wanting to admit to the feelings that were threatening to overwhelm him. That was the first time he'd wished anyone Happy Christmas in five years. Five long, horrible years.

What had he been doing? Had he been ignoring people around him like Karen and Molly for the last five years?

He heard an excited laugh and Grace walked through with one of the sales assistants from another room. Grace's cheeks were flushed pink with excitement and she was clapping her hands together again.

The girl really did love Christmas.

One part of him felt a selfish pang, while the other dared itself back into life. In a way, he'd felt better sticking his head in the sand for the last few years. Some of this Christmas stuff made him feel decidedly uncomfortable. Parts of it were making him relive memories—some good, some bad.

But the thing that he struggled most with was feeling again. *Feeling.*

The thing he'd tried to forget about.

He touched the saleswoman's arm as she was still mid-discussion with Grace. 'I need you to add something to the order.'

Grace's head shot up. 'What?' Then her expression changed. 'Really?'

He gave a nod and gestured to the white rocking horse. 'The lady in the dark coat, her name is Karen. Can you make delivery arrangements with her?'

The saleswoman shot a glance from Grace, to Finlay and then to Karen, who was still standing in the distance with Molly.

'Of course,' she said efficiently, adding the purchase to the bill.

What was he doing? All of a sudden Finlay was feeling totally out of his depth. 'Let's go,' he said to Grace abruptly.

She looked a little surprised but glanced at her watch. Did she think he wanted to beat the traffic? 'Thanks so much for your assistance. I'll be back at The Armstrong for the delivery.'

She rubbed her hands together again. Something sparked into his brain. The one thing he'd thought to do back at the hotel.

He pulled out his phone and spoke quietly as they hurried back outside to the car. The light had almost gone completely now and most of London's stores were lit up with Christmas displays. The journey to Harrods didn't take quite as long as he'd imagined.

Grace gave a sharp intake of breath as soon as the gold lights of the store came into view, lighting up the well-known green canopies.

He touched her elbow. 'We need to do something first in here before we go to the Christmas department.'

She looked surprised. 'Do you need some Christmas gifts for your family?'

He shook his head. Thick flakes of snow were falling outside. 'That's taken care of. This was something I should have done earlier.'

They stepped outside as the chauffeur opened the door and walked in through one of the private entrances.

A woman in a black suit with gold gilding met them at the entrance. 'Mr Armstrong?'

He nodded. She walked them towards some private lifts. 'This way, please.'

The journey only lasted a few seconds before the doors slid open on women's designer wear. Grace frowned and looked at him. 'We need to go to the Christmas department.'

He waved his hand. 'In a few minutes. I need to get something here first.' He turned to the personal shopper. 'Do you have anything the same shade as her shirt? And some black leather gloves please, lined.'

Grace was still frowning. 'Who is this for?'

He turned to face her. 'You.'

'What?' It was a face he recognised. Karen had worn the same expression thirty minutes earlier. 'What on earth are you talking about?'

Finlay held out his hands. 'Look at me. I've dragged you halfway across London in the freezing cold with snow outside.' He touched her arm. 'You're only wearing your suit and a shirt. You must be freezing. I feel like an idiot standing beside you in a wool coat.'

She tipped her head to the side. 'Then take it off. It's too hot in here anyhow.'

She said it so matter-of-factly. As if he should have thought of it himself.

He shook his head. 'But once we get back outside, you'll freeze again. You were rubbing your hands together the whole time we were in the last two stores. It was obvious you were still cold.'

The personal shopper appeared carrying a knee-length wool coat in the exact shade of pink as Grace's shirt. She held it up. 'Is this to your taste?'

He smiled. 'It's perfect.' He gestured towards the coat. 'Go on, Grace, try it on.'

She was staring at it as if she didn't quite know what to say. Then she shook her head. 'You are not buying me a coat.'

He took the coat from the personal shopper and held it open. 'You're right. I'm not buying you a coat. The Armstrong hotel is. Think of it as part of your official uniform.'

She slid her arms along the black satin lining of the coat as he pulled it up onto her shoulders. The effect was instant. The coat brought out the darkness of her chestnut hair and dark eyes while highlighting her pink cheeks and lips. It was perfect for her.

He felt himself hold his breath. Grace turned and stared at her reflection in a mirror next to them. Her fingers started automatically fastening the buttons on the double-breasted coat. It fitted perfectly.

The sales assistant brought over a wooden tray of black leather gloves. Grace stared down in surprise and looked up at Finlay. 'They're virtually all the same. How am I supposed to choose?'

The personal shopper looked dismayed. She started lifting one glove after another. 'This one only skims the wrist bones. This one has a more ruffled effect, it comes up much further. This one has a special lining, cashmere. We also have silk-lined and wool-lined gloves all at different lengths. Do you have a specific need?'

Finlay could tell by the expression on Grace's face that she was bamboozled. He reached out and ran his fingers across the gloves. Some instantly felt softer than others. He selected a pair and turned them inside out. 'These ones must be cashmere lined. The leather feels good quality too. Want to try them?'

He had no idea what size or length they were. Somehow he thought his eyes might be similar to Grace's—all the gloves looked virtually identical. But they didn't feel identical.

She slid her hands into the pair he handed her and smiled. 'They're beautiful...' She gave them a little tug. 'But they seem a little big.'

In an instant the personal shopper handed her

an alternative pair. Grace swapped them over and stretched her hands out. 'Yes, they feel better.'

'Perfect. Add this to our bill, please,' he said. 'We're going to the Christmas department.'

'But... I haven't decided yet.' Grace had her hand on the collar of the coat.

Finlay shrugged. 'But I have—the coat is perfect. The colour is perfect. The fit is perfect and the length is perfect. What else is there to say?'

He started to walk away but Grace wasn't finished.

'But maybe I'm not sure.' Her voice started to get louder as he kept walking, 'What if I wanted a red coat? Or a blue one? Or a black one? What if I don't even *like* coats?'

People near them were starting to stare. Finlay spun around again and strode back over to her, catching her by the shoulders and spinning her back around to face the mirror.

'Grace. This is you. This is your coat. No one else could possibly wear it.' He held his hands up as he looked over her shoulder.

Her dark brown eyes fixed on his. For a second he was lost. Lost staring at those chocolate eyes, in the face framed with chestnut tresses, on the girl dressed in the perfect rose-coloured coat.

There was a tilt to her chin of defiance. Was she going to continue to fight with him?

Her tongue slid along her lips as her eyes disconnected with his and stared at her reflection. 'No one has ever done something like this for me,' she whispered at a level only he could hear. She pulled her hand from the leather glove and wound one of her tresses of hair around her finger as she kept staring at her reflection.

'Just say yes,' he whispered back.

She blinked, before lowering her gaze and unwinding her finger from her hair. She pulled off the other glove and undid the buttons on the coat, slipping it from her shoulders.

She handed it to the personal shopper. 'Thank you,' she said simply, then straightened her bag and looked in the other direction. 'Right,' she said smartly, 'let's hit the Christmas department. We have work to do.'

She wasn't joking. The Christmas department was the busiest place in the entire store.

And Grace Ellis knew how to shop.

She left the personal shopper in her wake as she ping-ponged around the department, sidestepping tourists, pensioners, kids and hesitant shoppers.

He frowned as he realised she was picking only one colour of items. 'Really?' He was trying to picture how this would all come together.

She laid a hand on his arm as she rushed past. 'Trust me, it will be great.' Then she winked and blew into her fingers, 'It will be magical.'

She was sort of like a fairy from a Christmas movie.

He was left holding three baskets and feeling quite numb as she filled them until the contents towered. Lights. Christmas bulbs. Some weird variation of tinsel. A few other decorations and the biggest haul of snow globes. He hadn't seen one since he was a child.

'Really?' he asked again.

She picked up a medium-sized one and gave it a shake, letting the snow gently fall around the Santa's sleigh above a village. 'Everyone loves a snow globe…it's part of our theme.'

Our theme. She was talking about the hotel. Of course she was talking about the hotel. But the way her eyes connected with his as she said the words sent involuntary tremors down his spine. It didn't feel as if she were talking about the hotel.

Maybe this wasn't such a good idea after all. Maybe he should have started much smaller.

Grace's enthusiasm for Christmas had only magnified as the hours increased. Was he really ready for such a full-on Christmas rush?

She tugged at his sleeve. 'Finlay, I need you.'

'What?' He winced. He didn't mean for the response to be so out of sorts. The truth was, he wasn't quite sure what he was doing here, or how he felt about all this.

Five years ago he'd still been numb. Five years ago he'd spent September and October sitting by his wife's bedside. The year before that he'd been frantically searching the world over for any new potential treatment. On a bitter cold November day, he'd buried her.

Anna had been so much better than him at all of this. She'd been devastated by the news. Devastated by the fact no treatment had worked. But she'd been determined to end life in the way she'd wanted to. And that was at home, with her husband.

No one should have to watch the person they love fade a little day by day. But Finlay knew that every day the world over, there were thousands of people sharing the same experience he had.

Grace was standing in front of him, her face creased with lines. 'What's wrong?'

'Nothing.' He shook his head. 'Nothing. What do you need?'

She nodded to the snaking line in front of them. 'We've reached the front of the queue. I need you to pay.'

Pay. Something he could manage without any thought.

He walked to the front of the line and handed over the credit card. The personal shopper was putting all the purchases into some trolley for them to take to the car. He stopped her as she started to wrap the coat in tissue paper. 'Don't,' he said. 'Just take the tags off. Grace should wear it.'

There was a moment's hesitation on Grace's face as he handed the coat over. But after a few seconds she slid her arms back inside. 'Thank you.'

'No problem.'

By the time they got outside the air was thick with snow. It was lying on the pavements and surrounding buildings and roads.

Grace fastened her coat and slid her hands into the leather gloves while all their packages were stored in the boot of the chauffeur-driven car.

The journey back to the hotel was silent. He'd

started this afternoon with the hope of a little Christmas spirit. It wasn't that he wasn't trying. But sometimes memories flared. Tempering his mood with guilt and despair.

Grace's fingers fumbled over and over in the new gloves. She was staring at the passing shop windows. Her face serious and her eyes heavy. What was she thinking about?

When they reached the hotel he couldn't wait to get out of the car. 'I have an international video-conference,' he said as he climbed out.

'Good.'

He stopped mid-step. 'What?'

She walked around to the boot of the car. 'I don't want you to see anything until I've fin-ished. It's better if you have something to do. I'm going to get Frank and some of the other Maids in Chelsea to help me set things up. I'd prefer it if you waited until I was finished—you know, to get the full effect.'

It was almost as if somehow she had switched gears from her sombre mood in the car. Grace seemed back on point. Focused again. Ready to complete her mission.

And right now all he felt was relief. He could retreat into his office. He could stop asking himself why he'd bought a stranger's child a rocking horse and an employee a coat and gloves that were way outside her pay range.

Two of the doormen from the hotel started lifting all the purchases from the car. One of them gave her a nudge. 'Frank says there's a delivery at the luggage door for you.'

She was busy. She was engaged. She didn't need him around.

Finlay walked back through the reception without acknowledging anyone. He had work to do.

It was finished. It was finally finished. Grime and sweat had ruined her pink shirt and black skirt. She'd swapped back from the stilettos to her lower shoes and spotted a hole in her black tights. Her hair had ended up tied in a ponytail on top of her head as it kept getting in the way. She must look a complete state.

Emma gave a sigh as she looked up at the giant tree. 'If you'd told me this was what you had in mind when you asked for a hand...'

Sophie rolled her eyes. 'As if you would have said no.'

Ashleigh was leaning against the nearby wall

with her arms folded. 'I think it looks spectacular. It was worth it.'

Grace couldn't stop pacing. 'Do you think so? What about those lights over there? Should I move them?' She pressed her hands to her chest. 'What about the colour scheme? Is it too much?'

The girls exchanged amused glances.

But Grace couldn't stop with her pacing. 'I'll need to go and get him. I'll need to make sure that he's happy with it.'

Sophie walked over and put her arm around Grace's shoulder. 'Well, whoever *he* is, he'd be crazy if he didn't like this.'

Ashleigh stepped forward. 'I hope you've been paid for this, Grace. I'd hate to think this guy was taking advantage of your good nature.'

Emma folded her arms across her chest. 'Who is he, exactly? You haven't exactly been forthcoming.'

Grace hesitated. She wasn't even quite sure what to say. She tried to slip the question by giving Emma a big hug. 'Thank you for coming today. You're not even a Maid in Chelsea any more. Should I start calling you by your fancy title?'

But Emma was far too smart for that. She returned the hug then pulled back. 'I'm going to ask Jack if he knows anything about Finlay Armstrong.'

Grace shook her head—probably much too quickly. 'I don't think he will.' She turned and looked at the finished decorations again. 'I can't thank you girls enough. I owe you all, big time.'

'I think that's our cue to leave, girls,' said Ashleigh. 'Come on. Let's get cleaned up. I'm buying the drinks.'

They all gave Grace a hug and left by the main entrance of the hotel while she went to retrieve her jacket from behind the reception desk.

Should she wait? The hotel reception was quiet. She wasn't even sure of the time. She'd asked the staff to dim the main lights a little to give the full effect of the tree.

Her stomach gave a flip-flop. He'd asked her to do this. He'd asked her. Surely he'd want to see that she was finished?

She walked slowly towards his office door, listening out to see if he was still on his conference call. She couldn't hear anything and the office door was ajar.

She gave the door a gentle knock, sticking her head around it. Finlay was staring out of the window into the dark night. His office had a view of the surrounding area—not like the penthouse, of course, but still enough to give a taste and feel of the wealth of Chelsea. It was a wonder they didn't ask for credentials before they let you off the Tube around here.

He looked lost in his thoughts. She lifted her hand and knocked on the door again—this time a little more loudly.

He jumped. 'Grace.' He stood up; his actions seemed automatic. He started to walk around the desk and then stopped, the corners of his mouth turning upwards.

'What on earth have you done with your hair?'

She'd forgotten. She'd forgotten her hair currently resembled someone from a nineteen-eighties pop video.

She glanced down at her shirt too. Random streaks of dirt.

It wasn't really the professional look she'd been aiming for.

She gave her head a shake. 'I've been busy. This stuff doesn't put itself up.' Nerves and excitement were starting to get the better of her. 'Come and see. Come and see that you like it.'

He raised his eyebrows, the hint of a smile still present. 'You're already telling me I like it?'

'Only if you have exceptionally good taste,' she shot back.

He had no idea how much her stomach was in knots. This was the guy who hated Christmas. This was the guy that had pulled down a single strand of lights she'd put in his room.

This was a guy that was trying to take steps away from his past Christmas memories. If she'd got this wrong…

She stepped in front of him. 'It might be better if you close your eyes.'

'Nervous, Grace?' He was teasing her.

'Not at all.' She made a grab for his hand. 'Close your eyes and I'll take you outside. I'll tell you when you can open them.'

For a moment she thought he might refuse. She wasn't quite sure how long she could keep up the bravado. She stuck her hands on her hips. 'Hurry up, or I'll make you pay me overtime.'

He laughed, shook his head, took her hand and closed his eyes.

His hand in hers.

She hadn't really contemplated this. She hadn't

really planned it. His warm hand encompassed hers. Was her hand even clean?

The heat from his hand seemed to travel up her arm. It seemed to spread across her chest. She shouldn't be feeling this. She shouldn't be thinking thoughts like…

'Are we going?'

'Of course.' She gave his hand a tug and started walking—too quickly to begin with, then slowing her steps to a more suitable pace.

Magda at Reception raised her eyebrows as they walked past. Grace couldn't think straight for one second. This was it. This was where he would get the full effect. The effect that every customer walking into The Armstrong would get from now on.

She spun him around to position him exactly where she wanted him. Far enough away from the traditional revolving door at the entrance way to stop him getting a draught, but still with enough distance between him and the display.

She tapped his shoulder. 'Okay. Open your eyes.'

Maybe he'd been hasty. Maybe he shouldn't have made any of the suggestions about Christmas decorations. He didn't know what he was doing. He'd spent the last few hours trying to get the image of Grace in that pink coat out of his head.

He opened his eyes.

And blinked.

And blinked again.

His hotel was transformed. In a way he could never have imagined.

The lights in the main reception area were dimmed. In normal circumstances the black and grey floor, walls and reception desk would have made it as dark as night.

But it wasn't.

It was purple.

Purple in a way he couldn't even begin to find words for. He started to walk forward, straight towards the giant Christmas tree at the end of the foyer that was just pulling his attention like a magnet.

The traditional green tree was huge. It was lit up with purple lights and a few white twinkling ones. The large purple baubles and glass snowflake-style tree decorations reflected the purple light beautifully. The strange-style purple tinsel was wrapped tastefully amongst the branches. Along either wall were more purple lights. It was a strange effect. They drew you in. Drew your gaze and footsteps towards the tree. At intermittent points all along were snow globes of various sizes.

There was a choking noise beside him. Grace's face was lit up with the purple lights, her hands clenched under her chin and her eyes looking as if they might spill tears any second.

'What do you think?' Her voice was pretty much a squeak.

He couldn't speak yet. He was still getting over the shock.

Christmas had come to The Armstrong hotel.

She'd captured it. She'd captured the Christmas spirit without drowning him in it.

The tree was giant, but the effect of only having one colour made it seem more sleek and exclusive than he'd expected. The intermittent snow globes were focal points. Something people could touch, pick up and hold.

The dimmed lights were perfect. It bathed the whole area in the most magical purple light.

'Finlay?' This time there was a tremor in her voice.

He kept looking, kept looking at everything

around him, before finally turning and locking gazes with Grace.

'I think Santa got everything wrong,' he said.

Her eyes widened. 'What do you mean?'

Finlay laughed and opened his arms wide. 'His grotto. Clearly, it should have been purple.' He spun around, relishing the transformation of his hotel.

He didn't just like it. He loved it.

Never, even in a million years, did he think he'd feel like this.

He picked up Grace and swung her around.

She was still in shock. She put her hands on his shoulders and let out a squeal. She was still looking for verification. She needed to hear the words out loud.

'You like it? You think it's good?'

He set her feet back down on the slate floor. 'I don't think it's good—I think it's fantastic!' He shook his head. 'I can't believe you've done this. I can't believe you've managed to capture just what I wanted for The Armstrong without...'

His voice tailed off. That wasn't something to say out loud. That was part of his private thoughts.

She stepped in front of him again. This time

the tension on her face and across her shoulders had disappeared. The expression on her face was one of compassion, understanding. She touched his arm. 'Without taking you back to where you don't want to be.' She nodded. 'I wanted this to be about something new for you. Something entirely different.' She lowered her gaze. 'Not that there's anything wrong with memories. Not that there's anything wrong with taking some time.'

His heart swelled. He knew so little about Grace. This woman, that he'd almost threatened to fire, that had stood up to him, teased him, and shown him compassion and made him feel things he hadn't in years.

He was thinking things and feeling things that had been locked away inside for a long time.

He'd been so shut off. So determined not to let anything out—not to open himself up to the world of hurt that he'd felt before.

But things felt differently than he'd expected. The world outside didn't feel quite so bad as before. He recognised things in Grace that he hadn't expected to.

It was time to start making connections. Time to start showing interest in those around him. And he knew exactly where to start.

He reached down and took her hand. 'I owe you more than a coat.'

She shook her head automatically. 'No, you don't. And that coat is beautiful. Completely impractical and the kind of thing I wear in one of my dreams. Thank you for that.'

Her dark brown eyes met his. 'Every girl should get to be a princess some time.'

There was a little pang inside his chest. 'Come to the staff party with me.'

She dropped his hand. 'What?' She looked truly shocked.

'I mean it.'

Her mouth opened and then closed again.

'Every year there is a pre-Christmas staff party at the hotel. I haven't gone for the last five years. This year—it's time for me to attend again.' He shrugged. 'I can't promise I'll dance. I can't promise I'll play Santa Claus.' He gave her a serious nod. 'But I can promise you there will be music, spectacular food and champagne. If you want to be treated like a princess, then come to the party with me.'

She still looked a bit stunned. 'I've heard about the staff party. I just wasn't sure if I was going to go. What will the rest of the staff think if I go with you?'

He waved his hand. 'Who cares?'

'I care.' She looked serious.

He shook his head and took both her hands in his. 'Grace, they will think I'm saying thank you for the way you've decorated the hotel. The way you've managed to bring Christmas to The Armstrong in such a classy, stylish way. And they'd be right.'

She glanced over at the Christmas tree and finally smiled again.

She tilted her head to one side. 'Well, when you put it like that...'

CHAPTER FOUR

ALICE ARCHER COULD sniff out a problem from forty paces away. 'What's wrong with you today, Grace? One minute you're talking non-stop, next minute you're staring out of the window in some kind of daze. All with that strange expression on your face.'

Grace started back to attention. 'What expression?' she said quickly as she hung up another of Alice's coats.

Alice gave a knowing smile. 'That I'm-thinking-of-a-special-man kind of smile.'

Heat instantly seared her cheeks. 'I have no idea what you mean.'

But Alice wasn't put off. She merely changed the subject so she could probe another way. 'The decorations are beautiful.' She leaned back in her chair and gave a wistful sigh. 'I doubted I'd ever see Christmas in The Armstrong again. But you've captured the spirit perfectly.' She gave Grace a careful glance. 'Who knew that purple could be such a festive colour?' She picked up the individual snow globe that Grace had brought up to her room this morning, tipping it over so the snow swirled around in the liquid, then setting it back down on the table and watching it with a smile on her face.

'It's nice to see things changing.'

Grace was concentrating on the clothes hanging on the rails. She'd started arranging them into colour schemes. 'He's asked me to the staff party,' she said without thinking.

'He's what?'

Darn it. She'd played right into Alice's hands.

Alice pushed herself up from the chair and stood next to Grace. 'Finlay asked you to the party? He doesn't seem the type to do parties,' she added.

Grace turned to face her. 'He doesn't, does he?' She hadn't slept at all last night. The excitement of the day, the success of the decorations, the long hours she'd worked. The truth was she should have been exhausted and collapsed into bed. Instead, although her bones had been weary and welcomed the comfort of her bed, her mind had tumbled over and over.

Even though she'd been so busy, as soon as

she'd stepped inside the flat last night a wave of loneliness had swamped her. It had been there ever since her gran had died, but this time of year just seemed to amplify it. She'd ended up texting Clio and asking for extra shifts. She couldn't bear to be inside the house herself. Keeping busy was the only thing she could think of.

She wasn't quite sure how she felt about all this. Finlay had been straight with her. He was still mourning his wife. Christmas was hard for him. He was her boss. He'd been angry with her. He'd almost fired her.

But he hadn't felt like her boss on the roof when she'd been contemplating an even lonelier Christmas than she was already facing. For a few minutes he'd felt like someone she'd connected with.

Again, when he'd held her hand and those little tingles had shot straight up her arm.

Again, when he'd given her that look as he'd stood behind her in the shop and stared at their reflection in the mirror.

Again, when she'd seen joy on his face as he'd seen the purple Christmas decorations.

But she was probably imagining it all.

What did she know? When was the last time she'd been on an actual date?

Wait? Was this a date?

'He asked me to go to the party,' she said out loud again. 'It's only a thank you for the decorations.'

Alice gave a brief nod. 'Is it?' she said knowingly.

Grace made a little squeak. Panic was starting to wash over her. 'It's just a thank you.'

Alice turned and walked back to her chair. 'I don't know that he's ever taken anyone else to the party—or to *a* party.'

'No one else has done Christmas decorations for him,' Grace said quickly, sliding the doors closed on the wardrobe.

She had to stop overthinking this. He'd been clear.

'He said we might not even stay long. And he said he doesn't dance. But the food will be good and there will be champagne.'

Alice's smile grew broader. 'So, if you're not staying long at the party, what *exactly* are you doing?'

Grace replied automatically. 'I guess I'll just go home.' Her hand froze midway to the rubbish bag attached to her cart. Would she just be going home? Or would Finlay expect them to go somewhere else?

'What will you be wearing?'

'Oh, no!' Grace's hand flew to her mouth. She hadn't even thought of that. Her mind had been too busy trying to work out what an invite to a party meant. Her stomach in a permanent knot wondering how *she* felt about everything.

Truth was, there was no getting away from the fact that Finlay Armstrong was possibly the best-looking guy she'd ever seen.

That voice, those muscles, and those blue, blue eyes...

She swallowed and stuffed the rubbish in the bin. She'd seen women looking at him on their shopping trip. She'd seen the glances that already said, *What is he doing with her?*

Her mind did a quick brain-raid of her wardrobe. A black dress from a high-street store. A pair of skinny black trousers and fuchsia semi-see-through shirt. A strange kind of green dress with a scattering of sequins that she'd worn four years ago to a friend's wedding.

Nothing suitable for the kind of party she imagined it would be.

'I have no idea what I'll wear,' she said as she slumped against the wall.

Alice gave her a smile and tapped the side of her nose. 'Why don't you leave it with me? I don't have all my clothes in that wardrobe and I think I might have something in storage—' she glanced Grace up and down '—that might just be perfect.'

'Really?'

Alice smiled. 'Just call me the Christmas fairy. Come and see me on the day of the party.'

Finlay wasn't quite sure what he should be doing. His inbox had three hundred emails. There was a thick pile of mail on his desk. His PA had left some contracts to be reviewed. A few of his other hotels had staffing issues over Christmas. He'd also had an interesting email from Ailsa Hillier at the Corminster, asking how things were working out with her recommended company, Maids in Chelsea.

She'd probably already heard about the Christmas decorations. Someone at The Armstrong seemed to tell their rivals all they needed to know. Just as well it was a friendly rivalry. Ailsa had lost her sister to cancer some years ago and when Anna had died she'd sent a message with her condolences and telling Finlay she would take care of The Armstrong until he was ready to return. In the end, that had only been eight days—the amount of time it had taken to bury Anna—but he always remembered the kindness.

He picked up the phone, smiling as Ailsa answered instantly.

'I hear you've gone all purple.'

He choked out a laugh. 'It's a very nice colour.'

There was a moment's silence. 'I'm glad, Finlay. It's time.' Her voice was filled with warmth so the words didn't make him bristle. 'I might need to steal your designer though.'

Now he did sit straight in his chair. Ailsa couldn't possibly know about that, could she? He didn't give anything away. 'Your designer didn't pick purple this year?'

She sighed and he imagined she was putting her feet on the desk at this point. 'No. If they had then I could accuse you of copying. We are all white and gold this year and it already feels old. Tell me who you used and I'll poach them next year—after all, I did give you the Maids.'

He could sense she had a pen poised already. She was serious. And she didn't realise the connection. 'The Maids have worked out well, thank you. I'll ask Rob to have a look in the New Year about recruiting more permanent staff.' He leaned back in his chair. 'Or maybe I won't.' He drummed his fingers on the table as he thought. 'Some of our permanent residents seem to really like the Maids in Chelsea.'

'I think the truth is, Finlay, we get what we pay for. The Maids might cost more, but, in my experience, they are a polite, friendly, well-mannered bunch of girls. They want to do a good job and most of them seem to hide their light under a bushel. One of the girls I met yesterday has a degree in marketing, another has worked with four different aid agencies across four different continents. I like that.'

He liked that too. Hiding her light under a bushel seemed to fit Grace perfectly. The work she'd done here was great. Maybe it was time to find out a little bit more about the woman he'd invited to the staff party?

'You still haven't given me the name of the interior designer,' Ailsa reminded him.

He smiled. 'Her name is Grace Ellis, but you can't have her, Ailsa, she's all mine.'

He put down the phone with a smile, imagining the email he'd get in response.

He stood up and walked through to the main reception; Frank was just waving off some guests. 'Frank, do you know where Grace is?'

Frank gestured off to the left. 'Back down in the basement. She's had some more ideas.'

Finlay looked around. Even though it was daytime the decorations still looked good. He could smell something too, even though he had no idea what it was. It reminded him of walking into one of those winter wonderland-type places as a child.

Grace was still working on this? He'd have to pay her overtime. And bonuses.

He walked down to the basement. It was well lit and everything stored was clearly labelled. But that didn't help when he walked into the room he heard rustling in and found Grace upended in a large storage barrel. All that was visible was black kicking shoes and a whole lot of leg.

'Grace?' He rushed over to help.

'Eek! Finlay! Help.' He tried not to laugh as he reached inside the barrel and grabbed hold of her waist, pulling her out.

'Finlay,' she gasped again as she landed in a heap on the floor. Blue. She was wearing a blue shirt today. Not as cute as the pink one. But she'd just managed to lose a button on this one so he might like it even more. Her hair must have been tied with a black satin ribbon that was now trailing over her shoulder.

He burst out laughing. And so did Grace.

She thumped her hands on the floor. 'Well, *that* wasn't supposed to happen.' She followed the line of his vision and blushed, tugging at her skirt.

He peered into the barrel. 'What was supposed to happen?'

She pointed to the label. 'As I left the hotel last night I realised that although it was gorgeous when people walked inside, there was nothing outside. Frank told me there used to be lights outside. I was looking for them.'

He frowned, trying to remember what the lights had looked like. They'd been made by some American company and had cost a fortune. 'We did have. Is this where they've been stored? What makes you think they even work any more?'

She shrugged. 'I figured it was worth a try. I can always check them first. Then I was going to try and order some purple light bulbs—you know, carry the theme outside.'

Wow. She thought of everything.

He held out his hand to help her up. 'Grace, can I ask you something?'

He pulled a little harder than he should have, catapulting Grace right forward crashing into his chest. 'Oh, sorry,' she said, placing both hands on his chest. She looked up at him. 'What is it you want to ask?'

He couldn't remember. Not for a second. All he could concentrate on were the warm palms causing heat to permeate through his shirt. Grace lifted one finger. 'Oops,' she said as she stepped back.

Finlay looked down and sucked in a breath. Two hand prints on his white shirt.

To the outside world it would look amusing. To him?

A permanent imprint that he was in a place he wasn't quite sure of.

What exactly was he doing here? He'd deliberately come down here to find Grace. There was no point in him denying it to himself. He wanted to find out more about her. But was this a betrayal of Anna? He now had another woman's hands imprinted on his chest. And for a few seconds, he'd liked the feel of them being there.

He was exasperated. Exasperated that he was

drawn to this woman. Confused that he felt strangely protective of her. And intrigued by the person beneath the surface. There seemed to be so much more to Grace than met the eye. But how much did he really want to know?

Her hands were now clenched in front of her. He'd been quiet for too long.

'Finlay?'

He met her gaze. 'Are you free for lunch?'

'What?'

He glanced at his watch. 'Are you free for lunch?'

She looked down at her dishevelled clothing and pointed at his shirt. 'I don't think either of us can go anywhere like this.' He actually thought she looked fine.

He shrugged. 'I have other shirts.'

She shook her head. 'I only have what I'm wearing.' She bit her lip. 'But I think I might be able to borrow one of the bartender's black dresses.'

He gave her a nod. 'Five minutes, then?' He started to walk to the door.

'Finlay?' Her voice was quite serious.

'Yes?'

'Can I pick where we go?'

'Of course.' He was amused. He had no idea

where he'd planned to take her. His brain hadn't got that far ahead.

'See you in five, then.'

Grace was trying hard not to breathe. The only female bartender she could find was a size smaller. She'd managed to do up the zip on the dress but there wasn't much room. Lunch could be an issue.

Why had he asked her to lunch? Did he want to talk more decorations? And now she was late. After he'd left she'd grabbed the end of the lights to check they worked. They did.

Then she'd phoned a rush order for purple light bulbs. They would be delivered in a few hours. She'd need to find out how the lights normally got up there. This could be a disaster if she needed scaffolding. Maybe one of those funny little cherry pickers would do the trick?

Finlay was waiting for her at the front door. She tried not to notice the obviously interested looks they were getting from other members of staff.

She pulled down her woolly black sequined hat. She'd got it in the bargain bucket at the supermarket and it was the least likely match for her designer pink coat and gloves. But it was all she could afford at the time.

He smiled at her. He'd changed his white shirt for a blue one. Her stomach gave a little somersault. Yikes, it just made those blue eyes bluer.

'Where are we going?' he asked.

'What do you like for lunch?'

She still hadn't quite worked out why they were going for lunch. She assumed he wanted to talk about the decorations some more. And that was fine. But she intended on doing it somewhere she was comfortable.

'I'm easy.' He shrugged his shoulders. 'What do you like?'

They started walking along the street. 'Are you okay with the Tube?' she asked.

'You want to go someplace else?'

She licked her lips. 'I don't normally eat around here.' It was best to be upfront. There were lots of pricey and ultra-fashionable places to eat around here. Artisan delicatessens where a sandwich generally cost three times as much as it should.

She veered off towards the steps to the underground. Finlay just kept pace with an amused expression on his face. She pulled out her card to use while he fumbled around in his pockets for some change and headed for the ticket machine. She shook her head. 'Just scan your credit card. It will just deduct the payment.'

He frowned but followed her lead. They were lucky—a train had just pulled into the station. She held onto one of the poles and turned to face him as the train started to move. 'I'll give you a choice of the best breakfast around or some fantastic stuffed croissants.'

He looked at her warily. 'What, from the same place?'

She laughed. 'No, silly. They're two different cafés. I'm just trying to decide which one we go to.'

'I had breakfast at six. Let's go for the croissants.'

She gave him a solemn nod. 'I warn you—you might get angry.'

'Why?'

She stood on her tiptoes and whispered in his ear. 'Because the coffee in this place is *miles* better than it is in the hotel.'

She could see him bristle. 'No way.'

'Way.' The train slid to a halt. 'Come and find out for yourself.'

* * *

There was almost a skip in Grace's step as she led him from the Tube station and across the road to a café much like every other one in London. But as soon as he opened the door he could smell the difference. The scent of coffee beans filled the air, along with whiffs of baking—apple tarts, sponge cakes and something with vanilla in it. If you weren't hungry before you entered this café, you'd be ravenous ten seconds after crossing the threshold. He'd need to remember that.

They sat at the table and ordered. As soon as the waitress left, Grace started playing with a strand of hair. 'I might have done something,' she said hesitantly.

'What?' he asked cautiously.

'I might have ordered some purple light bulbs. And some white ones. I figure that if we can get the lights up outside the hotel it will give people an idea of what it looks like inside.'

He gave a nod. 'I had a call from the manager of another chain of hotels today. She was asking about you.'

Grace's eyes widened. 'Asking about me?'

He nodded. 'She wanted to know the name of

the designer I'd used because she'd heard how good the hotel looked.'

Grace leaned across the table towards him. 'Already? But I've only just finished.'

'I know that and you know that.' He held up his hand. 'But this is London, word travels fast.'

She shook her head. He could almost see her shrinking into herself. 'But I'm not a designer. I'm just one of the Maids in Chelsea.'

'We need to talk about that.'

'Why?'

Finlay reached into his jacket pocket and pulled out the cheque he'd written. 'I need to pay you for your services.'

Grace looked down and blinked. Then blinked again. Her face paled. 'Oh, no. You can't give me this.'

'Do you want to get Clio to bill me, then? I'm not sure why, though—this is different from the work you do for the agency.'

Her fingers were trembling. 'You can't pay me this much.'

Ah. He got it. It wasn't how he was paying her. It was how much he was paying her.

'I can increase it,' he said simply.

Her eyes widened even further. 'No.'

It almost came out as a gasp.

Ah. Now he understood.

'Grace, I based this on what we paid our last interior designer, plus inflation. That's all. As far as I'm aware, this is what I'd normally pay for these services.'

The waitress appeared and set down their plates. She'd caught the tail-end of the conversation—and glanced at the cheque under Grace's fingertips before making some kind of strangled sound.

Grace was looking distinctly uncomfortable. Finlay waved his hand and looked at the food in front of him. 'Take it, it's yours. You did a good job. You deserve it.'

He'd decided to follow Grace's lead. The croissant in front of him was stuffed with tuna and melted cheese. Salad and coleslaw were on the side and the waitress came back with steaming cups of coffee. She winked at him. 'Try the rhubarb pie after this, it's to die for.'

He almost laughed out loud. She'd seen the cheque and would expect a decent tip. He could do that.

'I think I might have to lie down after this,' he said, taking in all the food on the plate.

Grace was still watching the cheque as if it would bite her. He picked it up again and looked under the table, sliding it into her bag.

'Let's lunch.' He said the words in a way he hoped she'd understand. The amount wasn't open to debate. 'Where do you live?'

'What?' That snapped her out of her dream-like state. 'Why?'

He shrugged. 'I'd like to know a bit more about the woman I'm having lunch with.'

Didn't she want to tell him where she lived?

She lifted her knife and fork. 'I live in Waltham-stow,' she said quietly.

'Did you go to school around there?'

She nodded but didn't add anything further.

'How long have you worked for Maids in Chelsea?'

Her shoulders relaxed a little. That seemed a more acceptable question. 'Just for a few months.' She met his gaze, 'Truth is, it's the best job I've ever had. Clio, the boss, is lovely and the rest of the staff are like…family.'

Family. Interesting choice of word for work colleagues.

'What did you do before?'

She smiled. 'You name it—I've done it.'

He raised his eyebrows and she laughed. 'Okay, there are certain things I've never done. But I have had a few jobs.' She counted off on her fingers. 'I worked in the local library. Then in a few temp jobs in offices. I worked on the perfume counter of one of the department stores. Then I got poached to work on the make-up counter.'

'You got poached?' Somehow, he could see Grace with her flawless complexion and friendly personality being an asset to any make-up counter.

She nodded. 'But it wasn't really for me. I had to eventually give up due to some family issues and when I needed a job again Maids in Chelsea kind of found me.'

'Family issues? You have children?'

She shook her head and laughed. 'Oh, no. I'd want to find a husband first.'

He hadn't even considered the fact she might have children, or a husband! What was wrong with him? He tried to tease out a few more details. 'So, you haven't found a husband yet?'

She shook her head again. 'I haven't had time.' She looked up and met his gaze. 'I've dated casually in the last few years, but haven't really had time for a relationship.'

Due to her family issues? He didn't feel as though he could press.

'I take it you were brought up in Scotland?'

He smiled. 'What's the giveaway?'

She laughed and took a sip of her coffee. 'Is Sean Connery your father?'

'Sean Connery wouldn't have got a look-in. My mum and dad were childhood sweethearts. They lived next door to each other from the age of five.'

Grace set down her knife and fork. 'Oh, wow. That's so nice.'

It was nice. His mum and dad's marriage had always been rock solid, even when half the people he'd gone to school with seemed to have more step-parents than grades at school.

'Are they still in Scotland?'

'Always. They'll never leave.'

She gave him a fixed stare. 'Why did you leave?'

He hesitated then spoke quickly. 'Business.' There was so much more to it than that. He had a home—a castle—in Scotland that had been his pride and joy. He hadn't set foot in it for over a year. The penthouse in The Armstrong was where he now called home. He needed to change the subject—fast.

'Tell me about the Christmas stuff?'

She quickly swallowed a mouthful of food. 'What do you mean?'

He sipped his coffee. Then stopped and connected with her gaze. 'Wow.'

A smile spread across her face. 'I told you.'

He kept his nose above the coffee and breathed in the aroma, then took another sip. The coffee was different from most of the roasts he'd tasted. Finlay was a self-confessed snob when it came to coffee. This was good.

He looked over his shoulder to where the coffee machine and barista were standing. 'I have to find out what this is.'

She was still smiling. 'You'll be lucky if they tell you. The coffee in here has been this good for years. My gran and I used to come here all the time.'

Her voice quietened. He wanted to ask some more but it felt like prying. Could he really go there?

He went back to safer territory. 'The Christmas stuff. You seem to really enjoy it.'

She gave him a careful stare. Her voice was

soft. 'I do. I've always loved Christmas. It's my favourite time of year.' She stretched her fingers across the table and brushed them against his hand. 'I'm sorry, I know you said you didn't like it.'

He took a deep breath. The coffee was excellent in here. The food was surprisingly good. And the company…the company was intriguing.

Grace was polite, well-mannered and good at her job. She was also excellent at the unexpected job he'd flung on her the other day. She'd more than delivered.

It was more than a little distracting that she was also incredibly beautiful. But it was an understated beauty. Shiny hair and a pair of deep dark brown eyes that could hide a million secrets. But it wasn't the secrets that intrigued him. It was the sincerity.

Grace didn't feel like the kind of person who would tell lies. She seemed inherently good. All the staff at the hotel liked her. Frank was strangely protective of her.

He took a deep breath. 'It's not that I don't like it. I know I said that—'

She touched his hand again. 'No, you said you hated it.'

He nodded. 'Okay, I said I hated it. And I have. For the last five years. But I didn't always hate it. I had great Christmases as a kid. My sister and I always enjoyed Christmas with our mum and dad.'

Grace pressed her lips together. 'I've spent all my Christmases with my gran. My mum…' She paused as she searched for the words, 'My mum had me when she was very young. My dad was never on the scene. I was brought up by my gran.'

'Your mum wasn't around?'

Grace shook her head. 'Not much. She's married now—lives in Australia—and has a new family. I have two half-brothers.' Her gaze was fixated on her plate of food. 'She's very happy.'

'Do you talk?'

Grace looked up. 'Yes. Of course. Just…not much. We have a relationship of sorts.'

'What does that mean?'

Grace sighed and gave a shrug. 'I'm a twenty-eight-year-old woman. There's not much point in holding a grudge against someone who couldn't cope with a baby as a teenager. I had a good life with my gran. And we had the best Christmases together.'

He got the feeling she was taking the conversation away from her family circumstances and back onto Christmas.

'Is that where your love of Christmas came from?'

She smiled again and got a little sparkle in her eyes. 'Gran and I used to watch lots of black and white films, and we especially loved the Christmas-themed ones. We had a whole load of handmade ornaments. Spray-painted pine cones were our favourites. We did a lot of Christmas baking. We couldn't afford a real tree every year but we always had a holly wreath and I loved the smell.' There was something in her voice. Something in the tone. These were all happy memories—loving memories. But he could hear the wistfulness as she spoke.

He'd told her the biggest event in his life. It didn't matter that he'd blurted it out in anger with a whole host of other things. Grace knew probably the most important thing about him.

Him? He knew very little about her. It was like peeling back a layer at a time. And the further he peeled back the layers, the more he liked her.

She looked out of the window. 'I love Christmas—especially when it snows. It makes it just a little more magical. I love when night falls and you can look out across the dark city and see snow-covered roofs. I always automatically want to watch the sky to see if I can spot Santa's sleigh.'

'Aren't you a little old for Santa?' Her eyes were sparkling. She really did love the magic of Christmas. The thing that for the last five years he'd well and truly lost.

It made him realise how sad he'd been. How much he'd isolated himself. Sure, plenty of people didn't like Christmas. Lots of people around the world didn't celebrate it.

But, when it had been a part of your life for so long, and then something had destroyed it, the reminder of what it could be circulated around his mind.

She set down her knife and fork. 'Finlay Armstrong, are you telling me there's no Santa?' She said it in such a warm, friendly voice that it pulled him back from his thoughts without any regrets.

He pushed his plate away. 'Grace Ellis, I would *never* say something like that.'

She wagged her finger at him as her phone beeped. 'Just as well. In that case I won't need to tell you off.' She glanced at her phone. 'Oh, great, the light bulbs have arrived.' She reached around for her pink coat and woolly hat. Her eyes were shining again. 'Come on, Finlay. Let's light up The Armstrong!'

How on earth could he say no?

CHAPTER FIVE

'I HAVE THE perfect dress for you.' Mrs Archer clapped her hands together. 'You'll love it!'

'What?' Grace was stunned out of her reverie. She'd spent the last few days in a fog. A fog named Finlay Armstrong.

He'd managed to commandeer staff from every department and they'd spent two hours—Finlay included—replacing the light bulbs on the external display. Five specially phoned-in maintenance men had hung the purple and white strips down either side of the exterior of The Armstrong.

As they'd stood together on the opposite side of the street to get a better look, Finlay had given her a nudge. 'It does look good, Grace. You were right.' He took a deep breath. 'Thank you.'

The closed-off man who apparently had a reputation as a recluse was coming out of his shell. Except Finlay hadn't been in a shell. Grace got the impression he'd been in a dark cave where the only thing he'd let penetrate was work.

He was smiling more. His shoulders didn't seem quite so tense. Since their first meeting he'd never shouted, never been impolite. Only for the briefest second did she see something cloud his eyes before it was pushed away again. Even Frank had commented on the changes in the last few days.

She nudged Finlay back. 'Just wait until next year. I'll pick a whole new colour scheme and bankrupt you in light bulbs!' She'd been so happy, so excited that things had worked out she'd actually winked at him.

Winked. All she could do right now was cringe.

But the wink hadn't scared him off. Every time she'd turned around in the last two days, Finlay had been there—asking her about something, talking to her about other pieces of interior design work she might be interested in. Getting her to sit down and chat.

They'd had another lunch together. Around four coffees. And a makeshift dinner—a Chinese take-away in the office one night.

She'd even found herself telling him about the Elizabethan-style chairs she'd found in a junk shop and spent weeks re-covering and re-staining on her own.

Last night she hadn't slept a wink. Her brain had been trying to work out what on earth was going on between them. Was she reading this all wrong? Had it really been *that* long since she'd dated that she couldn't work out the signals any more?

'Ta-da!'

Mrs Archer brought her back to the present day by swinging open a cupboard door and revealing what lay behind it.

Wow.

It glimmered in the early-morning winter light. A full-length silver evening gown in heavy-duty satin with a bodice and wide straps glittering with sequins. Around the top of the coat hanger was a fur wrap. She was almost scared to touch it.

'Don't worry,' said Alice Archer. 'It's not real fur. But it probably cost ten times as much as it should.'

Grace's heart was pounding in her chest. She'd forgotten Alice had offered to find her something for the party. When Finlay had given her that exorbitant cheque the other day she'd almost squealed. Bills had been difficult since her grandmother had died.

Her grandmother and late grandfather had had

small pensions that had contributed to the upkeep of the flat. Keeping up with bills was tough on her own. There was no room for any extras—any party dresses. She'd actually planned on going to some of the charity shops around Chelsea later to see if she could find anything to wear tonight.

'It's just beautiful,' she finally said. Her hand touched the satin. She'd never felt anything like it in her life.

'The colour will suit you marvellously.' Alice smiled. 'I had it in my head as soon as you told me about the party.'

'When did you wear this, Alice? It's just stunning.'

Alice whispered in her ear. 'Don't tell Finlay Armstrong, but I wore it at a New Year ball in The Ritz the year my Robin proposed to me.'

Grace pulled back her hand. 'Oh, Alice, I can't wear your beautiful dress. It has such special memories for you—and it's immaculate. I would be terrified about something happening to it.'

Alice shook her head. 'Nonsense, I insist.' She ran her fingers down the fabric of the dress with a far-off expression in her eyes. 'I always think that clothes are for wearing. I think of this as my lucky dress.' She gave Grace a special smile. 'And I'm hoping it will bring you some luck too.'

Grace stared in the mirror. Someone else was staring back at her. Whoever it was—it wasn't Grace Ellis. Ashleigh had come around and set her hair in curls. Sophie had helped her apply film-star make-up. She'd never worn liquid eyeliner before and wasn't quite sure how Sophie had managed to do the little upward flicks.

Around her neck she was wearing the silver locket her grandmother had bought her for her twenty-first birthday and Emma had loaned her a pair of glittery earrings.

They were probably diamonds. But Emma hadn't told her that. She'd just squealed with excitement when she'd seen Grace all dressed up and said she had the perfect thing to finish it off.

And she'd been right. Right now, Grace Ellis felt like a princess. It didn't matter that the only items she was wearing that actually belonged to her were her locket, her underwear and her shoes.

The party was being held in one of the smaller main rooms in the hotel. The music was already playing and she could see coloured flashing lights. Her heart started beating in tempo with the music. Her hands were sweating. She was nervous.

But it seemed she wasn't the only one.

Finlay was pacing up and down outside the room. She couldn't help but smile. Just that one sight instantly made her feel better. Although the girls had helped her get ready they'd also plied her with questions.

'What's going on with you and Finlay Armstrong?'

'Is this a date?'

'Are you interested in him?'

'Do you want to date him?'

By the time they'd left her head had been spinning. She didn't know the answer to the first two questions. But the last two? She didn't want to answer them. Not out loud, anyway.

'Grace. You're here.' Finlay covered the distance between them in long strides, slowing as he reached her. At first he'd only focused on her face, but as he'd neared his gaze had swept up and down her body. He seemed to catch his breath. 'You look incredible.'

'You seem surprised.'

He shook his head. 'Of course I'm not surprised. You always look beautiful. But...' He paused and gestured with his hand. 'The dress and—' He reached out to touch the stole. 'What is this thing anyway? You look like a film star. Should I phone the press?'

He leaned closer, giving her a whiff of his spicy aftershave. She tried not to shiver. He tilted his head to the side. 'What have you done to your eyes?'

She touched his jacket sleeve. 'It's called make-up, Finlay. Women wear it every day.' She made a point of looking him up and down too. The suit probably cost more than she even wanted to think about. But it was immaculate, cut to perfection. 'You don't look so bad yourself.'

His gaze fixed on hers. 'Grace?'

'Yes?'

'Thank you for saying you'd come with me.' The tone of his voice had changed. He wasn't being playful now, he was being serious. 'You know I haven't come to one of these in the last few years.'

She licked her lips and nodded, trying not to let her brain get carried away with itself. 'Why have you come this year?' she asked softly.

She was tiptoeing around about him—trying not to admit to the rapidly beating heart in her chest. She liked this man a whole lot more than she should. She didn't even know what this was between them. But Finlay was giving her little signs of...something. Did he even realise that? Or was this all just in her imagination?

'It was just time,' he said, giving his head a little nod.

Her heart jumped up to the back of her throat. Time.

Just as it had been time to think about Christmas decorations. What else might it be time for?

The serious expression left his face and he stuck out his elbow towards her. 'Well, Ms Ellis, are you ready to go to The Armstrong's Christmas party?'

She slid her hand through his arm as all the little hairs on her arm stood on end. 'I think I could be. Lead the way.'

The party was fabulous. She recognised lots of faces. Other chambermaids, bar staff, porters, reception staff and kitchen staff. Frank the concierge had dressed as Father Christmas and looked perfect.

There was a huge table laid with appetisers and sweets. A chocolate fountain, a pick-and-mix sweetie cart and the equivalent of an outside street cart serving burgers.

Finlay nudged her. 'What? Did you think it would all be truffles and hors d'oeuvres?'

She gave him a smile. 'I wasn't sure.'

He shrugged. 'The first year it was. Frank discreetly told me later that the staff went home hungry. After that, I gave Kevin, from the kitchen, free rein to organise whatever he thought appropriate for the Christmas party. I don't think anyone has gone home hungry since.'

She laughed as he led her over to the bar. 'Which of the Christmas cocktails would you like?' he asked.

She was surprised. 'You have Christmas cocktails?'

'Oh, yes. We have the chocolate raspberry martini, the Festive Shot, with peppermint schnapps, grenadine and crème de menthe, then there is the Christmas Candy Cane, with berry vodka, peppermint schnapps and crème de cacao—or, my personal favourite, Rudolph's Blast: rum, cranberries, peach schnapps and a squeeze of fresh lime.'

Grace shook her head and leaned her elbows up on the bar. 'You know what's in every cocktail?'

He gestured to the barman. 'We'll have two Rudolph's Blasts, please.'

He leaned on the bar next to her and leaned his head on one hand. 'Okay, that dress. You kind of caught me by surprise. Where did you get it?'

She waved her hand. 'Did you expect me to come in uniform?'

He hadn't taken his eyes off her and the smile on his face—well, it wasn't just friendly. It seemed…interested. 'Of course I didn't. But you look like something the Christmas fairy pulled off the tree.'

Her eyes narrowed and she mirrored his position, leaning her head on one hand and staring straight back. 'And is that good—or bad?'

He didn't answer right away, and the barman set their cocktails down in front of them.

She leaned forward and took a sip of the cocktail. She licked her lips again as the mixture of rum and fruit warmed her mouth. He was focused on her mouth.

And she knew it.

She ran her tongue along her lips again then bit the edge of her straw.

'I only have the dress on loan,' she said quietly. 'And I've promised to take very good care of it.'

He leaned a little closer, obviously trying to hear her above the music playing around them. Had she lowered her voice deliberately? Maybe.

As he moved a little closer she was still focused on those blue eyes. Only they weren't as blue as normal. In the dim lights his pupils had dilated so much there was only a thin rim of blue around them. Was it the light? Or was it her?

'Who gave you the loan of the dress?'

'A good friend.'

'A designer?'

Ah…he was worried she'd been loaned the dress by a male designer. She could tell by his tone. She took another sip of her cocktail. It was strong. But it was warming lots of places all around her body. 'Someone much closer to home.'

His brow furrowed. She was playing games with him.

His hand reached over and rested on her arm. 'Someone I know?'

She smiled. 'Someone you respect. Someone I respect.' Grace lifted her hand and placed it on her chest. 'I'm told it's lucky. Her husband proposed to her when she was wearing this dress.'

Something flitted across his eyes. It was the

briefest of seconds but it made her cringe a little inside. That might have come out a little awkwardly. She wasn't dropping hints. She absolutely wasn't.

Then, it was almost as if the pieces fell into place. 'Alice Archer?' His voice was louder and the edges of his mouth turned upwards in a wide smile as he shook his head in disbelief, looking Grace up and down—again.

She was getting used to this.

'This was Alice Archer's dress?'

She nodded. 'This *is* Alice Archer's dress. She offered to give me something to wear a few days ago when she heard I was coming to the party.' Grace ran her palm across the smooth satin. Just the barest touch let her know the quality of the fabric. 'I had forgotten. When I walked in this morning she had it hanging up waiting for me.'

He moved closer again, his shoulder brushing against hers as he lifted his cocktail from the bar. 'Well, I think it's a beautiful dress. I have no idea how old it is, but it looks brand new.'

Her heart gave a little soar. The dress was definitely a hit. She'd need to buy Alice a thank-you present. A Christmas song started playing behind them, causing the rest of the people in the room to let out a loud cheer. The dance floor filled quickly. Grace sipped her drink.

'Do you want to dance?'

She shook her head. 'Not to this. I prefer to spectate when it's something wild. I prefer slow dances.'

She hadn't meant it quite to come out like that, but as her gaze connected with those blue eyes the expression on his face made her suck in a breath.

She could practically feel the chemistry between them sparkling. She wasn't imagining this. She just wasn't.

It wasn't possible for the buzz she felt every time he looked at her, or touched her, not to be real.

'I'll take you up on that,' he said hoarsely, before turning back to the barman. 'Can we have some more cocktails?'

His senses were on overload. Her floral scent was drifting around him, entwining him like a coiling snake. His fingertips tingled where they'd touched her silky skin. The throaty whisper of her voice had sent blood rushing through his body as if he were doing a marathon. His eyes didn't know whether to watch the smoky eyes, the tongue running along her succulent lips, the shimmer of the silver satin against her curves or the way her curls tumbled around the pale skin at her neck. As for taste? He could only imagine…

What was more, no matter how hard he tried, he couldn't shut his senses down.

It wasn't as if he hadn't spent time with women since Anna had died. On a few occasions, he had. But those encounters had been courteous, brief and for one purpose only.

There had been no attachment. No emotional involvement.

But with Grace? Things felt entirely different.

He wanted to see her. He wanted to be around her. He was interested in her, and what she thought. He didn't want to see her a few times and just dismiss her from his life.

It had been twelve years since he'd really dated. One date with Anna had been enough to know he didn't need to look any further. And right now, with his stomach tipping upside down, he wasn't sure he knew what to do any more.

Oh, he knew what to *do*.

He just couldn't picture doing it with emotions attached.

All of those memories and sensations belonged to Anna. He knocked back the last of the cocktail and lifted the Festive Shots that had appeared on the bar. He blinked, then tipped his back and finished it before turning to Grace.

Wow. Nope, nothing had changed in that millisecond. She was still here with her tumbling curls, sensational figure and eyes that looked as if they see down into his very soul.

She gave him a suspicious look as she eyed the shot glass. 'Who are you trying to get drunk, you, or me?'

He signalled to the barman again, who replaced his shot. He held it up and clinked it against her glass. 'This is only my third drink and it's only your second. Somehow, I think we can cope.'

She clinked her glass against his, then tipped back her head and downed her shot too. It must have hit the back of her throat because she laughed and burst out coughing. He laughed too and gave her back a gentle slap. 'It hits hard, doesn't it?'

She nodded as her eyes gleamed a little with water. 'Oh, wow.' She coughed again. 'Festive? More like dynamite.'

The music slowed and she glanced over her shoulder. 'Something you like?'

She tipped her head to the side as if she were contemplating the music. 'Actually, I really love this song.'

He didn't think. He didn't hesitate. He held his hand straight out to hers as Wham's Last Christmas filled the room. 'Then let's dance.'

She slid her hand into his. Her fingers starting at the tips of his, running along the palm of his hand and finishing as her fingers fastened around his wrist. His hand slid around her waist, skimming the material of the dress as they walked across the dance floor. He gave a nod to a few members of staff who nodded in their direction.

They were attracting more than their fair share of attention. He should have known this would happen. But the truth was, he didn't really care. This wasn't about anyone other than them.

Grace spun around as she reached the middle of the dance floor. Her hesitation only showed for a second before she slid her hands up around his neck.

It wasn't exactly an unusual position. This was

a Christmas slow dance. All around them people were in a similar stance. If they'd stayed apart it would have looked more noticeable.

He kept his hands at her waist as they moved slowly in time with the music. Grace was already singing along with her eyes half closed. 'Hey, isn't this a little before your time?'

Her eyes opened wider. 'Of course. But I don't care. I just love it. I loved the video even more. I watched it a hundred times as a teenager.'

Finlay wracked his brains trying to remember the video. For the first time he actually heard the words to the familiar tune. 'You like this? Isn't this the video where the girl dumped him and came back the next year with someone else?'

She threw back her head and laughed, giving him a delightful view of the pale skin at the bottom of her throat. His teeth automatically ground into his bottom lip. He knew exactly where he wanted his lips to be right now.

'Yes, that's the story. But I liked the snow in the video. It looked romantic. And I like the tune.'

Her body was brushing against his as she moved in time to the music. He pulled her a little closer as he bent to whisper in her ear. 'I can't believe this is your favourite Christmas song.'

She stepped back a little, grabbing his hand and twirling underneath it, sending the bottom of her silver dress spinning out around her, with the coloured lights from the disco catching the silver sequins on her bodice and sending sparkles around the room.

Her eyes were sparkling too, her curls bouncing around her shoulders. Grace was like her own Christmas decoration. When she finished spinning her hands rested on his chest.

He almost held his breath. Would she feel the beat of his heart under her fingertips? What would she make of the irregular pattern that was currently playing havoc with any of his brain processes—that must be the reason he couldn't think a single sane thought right now?

She finished swaying as his hands went naturally back to her hips. He could see a few staff members in the corner of the room looking at them and whispering. He might be the boss, but Grace worked with these people. She did a good job. She brought a little life into the hotel. She deserved their respect. He didn't want to do any-thing to ruin that.

As the music came to an end he grabbed hold of her hand and pulled her towards the exit. All of a sudden the room felt claustrophobic. There were too many eyes. Too many whispers. He didn't want to share Grace with all these people.

He wanted her to himself.

'Hey, Finlay—what's wrong?'

He leaned into the coat check and grabbed her stole, leaving some cash as a tip. He could hear Grace's feet scurrying behind him as he length-ened his stride to reach the exit as quickly as pos-sible.

They burst outside into the cold night air. He spun around and put the stole around her shoul-ders. She was breathing heavily; he could see the rise and fall of her chest in the pale yellow light of the lamp post above them. 'What are you doing?' Her voice was high. She sounded stressed.

He took a deep breath. He had no idea what he was doing. But could he really admit that?

He reached out and touched her cheek—just as he had on the roof that night.

'I needed to get out of there.'

He kept his finger against her cheek. It was the

slightest touch of her skin. The tiniest piece beneath his fingertip. But it was enough. Enough to set every alarm bell screaming in his brain. Enough to let his senses just explode with overload.

He was past the point of no return.

Grace reached up and captured her hand around his finger, leaving it touching her cheek. 'Why, Finlay? Why did you need to get out of there?'

He could hear the concern in her voice. She didn't have a clue. She thought this might be about something else. She didn't realise that every tiny part of this was about her.

Guilt was racing through his veins in parallel to the adrenaline. Feeling. He was feeling again. And the truth was that scared him.

Guys would never admit that. Not to their friends. Not even to themselves. But most guys hadn't loved someone with every part of their heart, soul and being and had it ripped out of them and every feeling and emotion buried in a brittle, cold grave.

Most guys wouldn't know that they didn't think it could be possible to ever get through that once. Why would they even contemplate making any kind of connection with another person when there was even the smallest possibility they could end up going down the same path?

Once had felt barely survivable. He couldn't connect with someone like that again. How could he risk himself like that again?

Where was his self-preservation? The barriers that he'd built so tightly around himself to seal his soul off from that kind of hurt again.

Somehow being around Grace had thrown his sense of self-preservation out of the window. All he could think about right now was how much he wanted to touch and taste the beautiful woman in front of him.

She was still watching him with those questioning brown eyes. She was bathed in the muted lamplight—her silver dress sparkling—like an old-fashioned film star caught in the spotlight.

He stopped thinking. 'Because I couldn't wait to do this.'

He pulled her sharply towards him, folding his arm around her waist and pulling her tightly against the length of his body. He stopped for a second, watching her wide eyes, giving her the briefest of pauses to voice any objections. But there were none.

He captured her mouth in his. She tasted of

cocktails and chocolate. Sweet. Just the way he'd imagined she would. One hand threaded through her tumbling curls and the other rested on the satin-covered curve of her backside. He'd captured his prize. He wasn't about to let her go.

After two seconds the tension left her body, melding it against his. Her hands wound their way around his neck again, her lips responding to every part of the kiss, matching him in every way.

This was what a connection felt like. He hadn't kissed a woman like this since Anna died. This was what it felt like to kiss a woman you liked and respected. It had been so long he hadn't even contemplated how many emotions that might toss into the cold night air.

Her hand brushed the side of his cheek, running along his jaw line. He could hear the tiny scrape of his emerging stubble against her fingernails. The other hand ran through his hair and then down to his chest again. He liked the feel of her palm there. If only it weren't thwarted by the suit jacket and shirt.

Their kiss deepened. His body responded. He knew. He knew where this could potentially go.

Grace pulled her lips from his. It was a reluctant move, followed by a long sigh. Her forehead rested against his as if she were trying to catch her breath. He could feel her breasts pressed against his chest.

His hand remained tangled in her soft hair and for a few moments they just stood like that, heads pressed together under the street light.

He eventually straightened up. Should he apologise? It didn't feel as if the kiss was unwanted. But they were right in the middle of the street— hardly the most discreet place in the world for a first kiss. He could ask her up to the penthouse but somehow that didn't feel right either—and he was quite sure Grace wouldn't agree to come anyway.

'Thank you for coming tonight,' he said quietly.

Her voice was a little shaky. 'You're welcome.'

He took a step back. 'How about I get one of the chauffeurs to drop you home?'

He had no idea what time it was—but whatever time it was, he didn't want her travelling home alone. He trusted all the chauffeurs from The Armstrong. Grace would be in safe hands.

She gave a little nod. 'That would be nice, thank you.' This time her voice sounded a little odd. A little detached. Had she rethought their kiss and changed her mind?

He put his arm behind her and led her back to the main entrance of the hotel, nodding to one of the doormen. 'Callum, can you get one of the chauffeurs to take Grace home?'

She shivered and pulled the stole a little closer around her shoulders. 'Do you want me to get you another coat?'

She shook her head, not quite meeting his gaze. 'I'll be fine when I get in the car. That'll be warm enough.'

For a couple of minutes they stood in awkward silence. Finlay wasn't quite sure what to do next. He wasn't quite sure *what* he wanted to do next. And he couldn't read Grace at all.

The sleek black car pulled up in front of them and the driver jumped out to open the door. Grace turned to face him with her head held high. 'Thank you for a lovely evening, Finlay,' she said as she climbed into the car.

'You too,' he replied automatically as he closed the door, and watched the car speed off into the distance.

One thing was for sure. Finlay Armstrong wouldn't sleep a wink tonight.

CHAPTER SIX

SHE COULDN'T DESCRIBE the emptiness inside her. It was impossible to put into words.

She stared at the texts on the phone from her friends, teasing her about the party and assuming she'd had the time of her life.

She had—almost.

But last night when she'd opened the door to the cold and empty flat, everything had just overwhelmed her.

Silence echoed around her.

Unbearable silence.

The home that had once been filled with love and happiness shivered around her.

She actually felt it happen.

Even when she flicked the light switch, the house was dark. Emptiness swamped every room. She'd started to cry even before she'd made it to bed, wrapping herself in her gran's shawl, her own duvet and wearing the thickest pair of flannel pyjamas imaginable—but nothing could keep out the cold. Nothing at all.

That feeling of loneliness was enormous. Somewhere, on the other side of the planet, her mother was probably cuddled up to her husband or sitting around a table with her two children. Children she actually spent time with.

It wasn't that she didn't understand. Getting pregnant at sixteen would be difficult for any teenager. But to move away completely and form a new life—without any thought to the old—was hard to take.

It made her more determined. More determined to never feel second best with any man. She'd spent her whole life feeling second best and a cast-off. Although her relationship with her gran had been strong and wonderful, there had still been that underlying feeling of…just not being enough.

For the briefest spell tonight, under that lamp post, she'd felt a tiny bit like that again. All because of that kiss. Oh, the kiss had been wonderful—mesmerising. The attraction was definitely there. But the connection, or the sincerity of the connection? She just couldn't be sure if when Finlay kissed her he was thinking only of her.

She shivered all night. The heating was on in the flat and it didn't matter how high the temperature was —it just couldn't permeate her soul.

The night with Finlay had brought things to a precipice in her head.

Alone. That was how she felt right now.

Completely and utterly alone.

She'd thought being busy at Christmas would help. She'd thought decorating the flat the way it always used to be would help.

But the truth was nothing helped. Nothing filled the aching hole that her grandmother's death had left.

A card had arrived from her mother. The irony killed her. It was a personalised card with a photo of her mum with her new husband, Ken, and their two sons on the front. They were suitably dressed for a Christmas in Florida. It wasn't meant to be a message. But it felt like it.

Her mother had moved on—playing happy families on another continent. She'd found her happy ever after. And it didn't include Grace. It never had.

She received the same store gift card each year. Impersonal. Polite. The sort of gift you sent a colleague you didn't know that well—not the sort of gift you sent your daughter.

As she rode the Tube this morning people seemed to be full of Christmas spirit. It was Christmas Eve. Normally she would be full of Christmas spirit too.

But the sight of happy children bouncing on their parents' knees, couples with arms snaked around each other and stealing kisses, only seemed to magnify the effect of being alone.

Tonight, she'd go home to that dark flat.

Tonight, she'd spend Christmas Eve on her own. There was no way she could speak to any of the girls. They were all too busy wrapped up in their own lives, finding their own dreams, for Grace to bring them down with her depressed state.

The train pulled into the station and she trudged up the stairs to work.

This time last year her stomach had been fluttering with the excitement she normally felt at Christmas. Christmas Eve was such a special day.

It was for love, for families, for sharing, for fun and for laughter. Tomorrow, she would probably spend the whole day without speaking to a single person. Tomorrow, she would cook a dinner for one.

She'd pushed away every single thought about how she might spend Christmas Day. It had been easier not to think about it at all. That way she could try and let herself be swept along with the spirit of Christmas without allowing the dark cloud hanging above her head to press down on her.

But now, it seemed to have rushed up out of nowhere. It was here and the thought of being alone was just too much.

She pulled her phone out of her pocket and dialled. 'Clio? Are there any shifts tomorrow?'

She could almost hear the cogs whirring in Clio's brain at the end of the phone. 'Grace? What's wrong?'

Grace sucked in a deep breath to try and stop her voice from wobbling. She couldn't stop the tears that automatically pooled in her eyes. 'It's just the time of year…it's hard,' she managed.

'Your gran. You're missing her. I get it. But do you really want to spend Christmas Day working?' The compassion in Clio's voice made her feel one hundred times worse.

'Yes.'

There was a shuffle of papers. 'You can work at The Armstrong as normal. There are always lots of shifts at Christmas. I can put you on for that one.'

'Great, thanks.' The words came out easier this time; it was almost as if a security blanket had been flung over her shoulders. 'And, Clio? Congratulations on your engagement. Enjoy your time with Enrique.'

She hung up the phone and sighed. She meant it. She really did. Clio was over the moon with her new relationship and she deserved to be happy.

She changed quickly and started work. The Christmas themed music that she'd chosen was playing quietly in the background *everywhere.*

Other members of staff were smiling and whistling. No one was rushing today. The whole work tempo seemed to have slowed down for the festive season. And Grace noticed a few sideways glances from people who'd attended the staff party.

Her list was long. Lots of people had the day off. But Grace didn't care; it would keep her busy and give her less time to think.

It was surprising the amount of guests who checked in and out around Christmas. Something panged inside her again. People coming to visit families and friends.

Eight hours later her hair was back to its semi-normal dishevelled state and she really wanted to get changed. One of the staff called her over. 'Can you do one more before you knock off tonight? I'm in a bit of a rush.'

Grace pressed her lips together. She knew Sally had four kids and would want to get home to them early. She held out her hand. 'Of course I will. No problem.'

Sally gave her a hug. 'Thanks, Grace. Have a great Christmas.'

Grace glanced at the list and her stomach did a little flip-flop. She had The Nottingdale Suite to clean—Finlay's place. She glanced towards the office. He'd be in there right now. If she was quick—she could get things done and get back out before he knew she was working.

It was a weird feeling. When he'd held her in his arms last night she'd felt…she'd felt…special. A tiny little fire that had been burning inside her for the last few days had just ignited like a firework—only to sputter out again.

The Nottingdale Suite didn't feel quite so empty as before. One of her Christmas snow globes was sitting on the main table, with a wrapped parcel on the slate kitchen worktop.

Grace couldn't help but pick it up. It was intricately wrapped in silver paper with curled red ribbon and a tag. The writing was copperplate. Grace smiled. She recognised it immediately and set it down with a smile. Mrs Archer had left a present for Finlay. How nice.

She made short work of cleaning the penthouse. The bathroom, kitchen area, bedroom and lounge were spotless in under an hour.

She stared out for a second over the dark London sky. In a few hours Christmas Eve would be over. By the time she got home, she could go straight to bed then get up early for her next shift. She squeezed her eyes closed for a second.

Please just let this Christmas be over.

'Grace?' She was the last person he expected to see at this time of night. 'What are you doing?'

The words were out before he even noticed the cart next to the doorway.

She jumped and turned around. 'Finlay.' The words just seemed to stop there.

She was wearing her uniform again. But in his head she still had on the silver dress from the last night. That picture seemed to be imprinted on his brain. Seared on it, in fact.

She still hadn't spoken. The atmosphere was awkward.

He wasn't quite sure how to act around Grace.

That kiss last night had killed any ounce of sleep he might have hoped to get.

His brain couldn't process it at all. There was no box to put it in.

It wasn't a fleeting moment with someone unimportant. It hadn't been a mistake. It wasn't a wild fling. It hadn't felt casual. So, what did that leave?

Grace's eyes left his and glanced at the outside view again—exactly where she'd been staring when he came in. He heard a stilted kind of sigh. She moved over towards the cart.

This wasn't going to get any easier. Neither of them seemed able to do the casual and friendly hello.

He had a freak brainwave. This was Christmas Eve. Grace was the woman that loved Christmas. No—she lived and breathed Christmas. What on earth was she doing still working?

Grace picked up some of the cleaning materials and shoved them back in her cart. 'Merry

Christmas, Finlay.' The words were stilted. Was this how things would be now?

'Merry Christmas, Grace.' His response was automatic. But something else wasn't.

The feelings that normally washed around a response like that. Normally they were cold. Harsh. Unfeeling and unmeant.

This was the first time in five years he'd actually meant those words as he said them.

He wanted Grace to have a merry Christmas. He wanted her to enjoy herself.

What if...?

The idea came out of nowhere. At least, that was how it seemed. He was flying back to Scotland on Boxing Day to see his family. Chances were, this would be the last time he would see Grace between now and then.

There were a dozen little flashes in his brain. Grace on the roof. Touching the tear that had rolled down her cheek. Drinking hot chocolate with her. The gleam in her eyes when she was cheeky to him. The expression on her face when she'd tried on the pink coat. The wash of emotions when he'd spotted the little girl and bought the rocking horse for her Christmas. Grace's ruffled hair and pushed-up shirt as she'd wound in hundreds of purple bulbs. The way she'd clapped her hands together when he'd first seen the tree.

And the feel of her lips on his. Her warm curves against his. The soft satin of her dress under the palm of his hand.

He'd felt more alive in the last week than he had in the last five years.

And that was all because of Grace.

He reached out to touch her arm. 'It's been nice to meet you. Enjoy Christmas Day.'

The words were nowhere near adequate. They didn't even begin to cover what he wanted to say or what was circulating in his brain.

Grace's dark brown eyes met his. For a second he thought she was going to say the same thing. Then, her bottom lip started to tremble and tears welled in her eyes. 'I'll be working as normal.'

He blinked. What?

Why would the girl who loved Christmas not be spending it with her family and friends?

'What do you mean—you're working? Don't you have plans with those you love?'

As soon as the words were out he realised he'd said exactly the wrong thing. The tears that had pooled in her eyes flooded over and rolled down her cheeks.

He reached out his arms to her. 'What on earth's wrong? Grace? Tell me?'

She was shaking and when the words came out it was the last thing he expected.

'There's no family. My gran…she died…she died a few months ago. And now, there's just no one. I can't face anything.' She looked at him, her gaze almost pleading. 'I thought I could do this. I thought I could. I thought if I kept busy and kept working everything would just fall into place. I wouldn't have time to miss her so much.' She kept shaking her head. 'But it's harder than I could ever imagine. Everywhere I go, everywhere I look, I see people—families together, celebrating Christmas the way I used to. Even Mrs Archer—I love her—but I'm finding it so hard to be around her. She reminds me so much of my gran. The way she speaks, her mannerisms, her expressions.' She looked down as she kept shaking her head. 'I just want this to be over.' Now, she looked outside again into the dark night. In the distance they could see the Christmas red and white lights outlining Battersea Power Station. 'I just want Christmas to be over,' she breathed.

Every hair on his arms stood on end. He got it. He got all of it.

The loneliness. The happy people around about, reminding you of what you'd lost. The overwhelming emotions that took your breath away when you least expected it.

He put his hands on her shoulders. 'Grace, you don't need to be here. You don't need to work at Christmas. It's fine. We can cover your shifts. Take some time off. Get away from this. The last thing you want to do is watch other families eating Christmas dinner together. Stay home. Curl up in bed. Eat chocolate.'

It seemed like the right thing to say. Comfort. Away from people under her nose.

But Grace's eyes widened and she pulled back. 'What? No. You think I want to be alone? You think I want to spend the whole of Christmas without talking to anyone, without seeing another living soul? Do you think anything looks worse on a plate than Christmas dinner for one?'

As she spoke he cringed. What he'd thought might take her away from one type of agony would only lead her to another. He hated this. He hated seeing the pain in her eyes. The hurt. The loneliness. He recognised them all too well. He'd worn the T-shirt himself for five years.

He squeezed her shoulders. 'Then what is it you

want for Christmas, Grace? What is it you want to do? What would be your perfect Christmas?'

His agitation was rising. She'd got herself so worked up that her whole body was shaking. He hated that. He hated she was so upset. Why hadn't he realised she was alone? Why hadn't he realised she was suffering a bereavement just as he was?

Grace had always been so upbeat around him, so full of life that he'd missed the signs. He knew better than most that you only revealed the side of you that you wanted people to see.

He'd been struck by Grace's apparent openness. But she'd built the same guard around her heart as he had. It didn't matter that it was different circumstances. This year, she felt just as alone as he had over the last five.

He didn't want that for her. He didn't want that for Grace.

What if...?

The thought came out of nowhere. He didn't know quite what to do with it.

Her eyes flitted between him and the outside view. 'Tell me, Grace. Tell me what your ideal Christmas would be. What do you want for Christmas?' His voice was firm as he repeated his question. The waver in her voice and tears had been too much for him. Grace was a kind and good person. She didn't deserve to be lonely this Christmas. He had enough money to buy just about anything and he was willing to spend it to wipe that look off her face.

Her mouth opened but the words seemed to stall.

'What?' he prompted gently.

'I want a proper Christmas,' she breathed. 'One with real snow, and a log fire, and a huge Christmas turkey that's almost too big to get in the oven.' She took a deep breath. 'I want to be able to smell a real Christmas tree again and I want to spend all day—or all night—decorating it the way I used to with my gran. I want to go into the kitchen and bake Christmas muffins and let the smell drift all around.' She squeezed her eyes closed for a second. 'And I don't want to be alone.'

Finlay was dumbstruck. She hadn't mentioned gifts or 'things'. Grace didn't want perfume or jewels. She hadn't any yearning for materialistic items.

She wanted time. She wanted company. She wanted the Christmas experience.

He glanced out of the window again. He was a little confused. Snow dusted the top of every rooftop in London—just as it had for the last week.

'What do you mean by snow?' he said carefully.

She opened her eyes again as he released his hands from her shoulders. She held out her hands. 'You know—real snow. Snow that's so thick you can hardly walk in it. Snow you can lie down on and do snow angels without feeling the pavement beneath your shoulder blades. Snow that there's actually enough of to build a snowman and make snowballs with. Snow that, when you look out, all you can see is white with little bumps and you wonder what they actually are.' He could hear the wonder in her voice, the excitement. She'd stopped being so sad and was actually imagining what she wished Christmas could be like.

'And then you go inside the house and all you can smell is the Christmas tree, and the muffins, and then listen to the crackle of the real fire as you try and dry off from being outside.' She was smiling now. It seemed that Grace Ellis could tell him exactly what she wanted from this Christmas.

And he knew exactly where she could get it. The snow scene in her head—he'd seen that view a hundred times. The crackling fire—he had that too.

This was Grace. The person who'd shot a little fire into his blood in the last few days. The person who'd made him laugh and smile at times. The girl with the warm heart who had let him realise the future might not be quite as bleak as he'd once imagined.

He could do this. He could give her the Christmas she deserved.

'Pack your bag.'

Her eyes widened and she frowned. 'What?'

He started walking through the penthouse, heading to his cupboards to pull out some clothes. It was cold up north; he'd need to wrap up.

'I'll take you home to grab some things. I can show you real snow. I can light a real fire. We can even get soaked to the skin making snow angels.' He winked at her. 'Once you've done it—you'll regret it.'

Grace was still frowning. 'Finlay, it's after eight o'clock on Christmas Eve. Where on earth are you planning on taking me? Don't you have plans yourself?'

He shook his head as he pushed some clothes in a black bag. 'No. I planned on staying here and going up on Boxing Day to visit my parents and sister. My helicopter is on standby. We can go now.'

She started shaking her head. 'Go where?'

'To Scotland.'

CHAPTER SEVEN

THINGS SEEMED TO happen in a blur after that.

Her cart abandoned, Finlay grabbed her hand and made a quick phone call as they rode down in the elevator. The kitchen was still busy and it only took two minutes for him to corner the head chef.

'I need a hamper.'

The head chef, Alec, was in the middle of creating something spectacular. He shot Finlay a sharp look, clearly annoyed at being interrupted.

'What?'

But enthusiasm had gripped Finlay. 'I need a hamper for Christmas. Enough food for dinner tomorrow and all the trimmings.' He started opening the huge fridges next to Alec. 'What have you got that we can take?'

Grace felt herself shrink back. Alec was clearly contemplating telling Finlay where to go. But after a few seconds he gestured to a young man in the corner. 'Ridley, get one of the hampers from the stock room. See what we've got to put in it. Get a cool box too.'

Finlay had started stockpiling everything he clearly liked the look of on one of the counters where service was ongoing. The staff were dodging around them as they tried to carry on. She moved next to his elbow. 'I think we're getting in the way,' she whispered.

Prosciutto ham, pâté, Stilton and Cheddar cheese, oatcakes, grapes and some specially wrapped chocolates were already on the counter. Finlay looked up. 'Are we?' He seemed genuinely surprised about the chaos they were causing. 'What kind of wine would you like?' he asked. 'Or would you prefer champagne?'

Alec caught sight of her panicked face. He leaned over Finlay. 'Where exactly are you going?'

'Scotland.' It was all she knew.

Alec didn't even bat an eyelid, he just shouted other instructions to some of the kitchen staff. 'Louis, find two large flasks and fill them with the soups.'

Finlay still seemed oblivious as he crunched on a cracker. 'What are the soups?'

Alec didn't even glance in his direction; he

was scribbling on a piece of paper. 'Celeriac with fresh thyme and truffle oil, and butternut squash, smoked garlic and bacon.'

A wide smile spread across Finlay's face. 'Fantastic.'

Ridley appeared anxiously with the hamper already half filled and looked at the stack of food on the counter. He started moving things between the hamper and cool box.

'Christmas pudding,' said Finlay. 'We need Christmas pudding.' Ridley glanced over at Alec, who let out a huge sigh and turned and put one hand on his hip and thrust the other towards Finlay.

Finlay frowned as he took the piece of paper. Alec raised his eyebrows. 'It's instructions on how to cook the turkey that's just about to go in your cool box.' He gave Grace a little smile, 'I'd hate it if you gave the lovely lady food poisoning.'

Finlay blinked then stuffed the paper into the pocket of his long black wool coat. 'Great. Thanks.'

Louis appeared with the soup flasks and some wrapped bread.

'We'll grab the wine on the way past. Is there anything else you want, Grace?'

She shook her head. Had she actually agreed to go to Scotland with Finlay? She couldn't quite remember saying those words. But somehow the dark cloud that had settled over her head for the last day seemed to have moved off to the side. Her stomach was churning with excitement. Finlay seemed invigorated.

A Christmas with real snow? It would only be a day—or two. He was sure to want to get back to work straight away. And the thought of a helicopter ride…

'Grace, are we ready?' He had the hamper in one hand and the cool box in the other.

She nodded.

It seemed as though she blinked and the chauffeur-driven car pulled up outside her flat. Her hand hesitated next to the door handle. This part of London was nowhere near as plush as Chelsea. She felt a little embarrassed to show Finlay her humble abode.

But his phone rang and he pulled it from his pocket. She slid out of the car. 'I'll be five minutes.'

He nodded as he answered the call and then put his hand over the phone. 'Grace?'

She leaned back in. 'What?'

He winked. 'Bring layers.'

She was like a whirlwind. Throwing things into a small overnight case, grabbing make-up and toiletries and flicking all the switches off in the house. She flung off her clothes and pulled on a pair of jeans, thin T-shirt, jumper and some thick black boots. The pink coat was a must. He'd bought it for her and it was the warmest thing that she owned.

She grabbed her hat, scarf and gloves and picked up the bag.

Then stopped to catch her breath.

She turned around and looked inside at the dark flat. The place she'd lived happily with her grand-mother for years. This morning she'd been cry-ing when she left, dreading coming home tonight. Now, the situation had turned around so quickly she didn't know which way was up.

The air was still in the flat, echoing the emp-tiness she felt there now. 'Love you, Gran,' she whispered into the dark room. 'Merry Christmas.'

She closed the door behind her. This was about to become the most unusual Christmas ever.

Grace squealed when she saw the helicopter and took so many steps backwards that he thought she might refuse to fly. He put his arm around her waist. 'Come on, it's fine. It's just noisy.'

Her steps were hesitant, but he knew once she got inside she would be fine. The helicopter took off in the dark night, criss-crossing the bright lights of London and heading up towards Scotland.

Once she'd got over the initial fear of being in the helicopter Grace couldn't stop talking. 'How fast does this thing go? Do we need to stop anywhere? How long will it take us to get there?' She wrinkled her nose. 'And where is *there*? My geography isn't great. Whereabouts in Scotland are we going?'

He laughed at the barrage of questions. 'We need to fly around three hundred and eighty miles. Yes, we'll need to stop to refuel somewhere and it'll take a good few hours. So, sit back, relax and enjoy the ride.'

Grace pressed her nose up next to the window for a minute. But she couldn't stop talking. It was clear she was too excited. 'Where are we going to stay? Will your family be there? Can I decorate again, or will they already have all the decorations up?'

Finlay sucked in a breath. His actions in the

heat of the moment had consequences he hadn't even considered. His parents weren't expecting him until Boxing Day. He hadn't even called them yet—and now it was after ten at night. Hardly time to call his elderly parents. His sister was staying. He knew there was his old room. But there weren't *two* spare rooms. And his parents would probably jump to an assumption he didn't want them to.

This could be awkward.

He gulped. Not normal behaviour for Finlay. His brain tried to think frantically about the surrounding area. Although he stayed in the country they weren't too far away from the city. There were some nice hotels there. And, if he remembered rightly, there were some nice hotels in the surrounding countryside area.

He pulled out his phone to try and do a search. 'I haven't booked anywhere,' he said quickly as he started to type. 'But I'm sure we can find a fabulous hotel to stay in.'

'A hotel?' It was the tone of her voice.

'Yes.' His fingers were still typing as he met her gaze and froze.

'We're going to *another* hotel?'

It was the way she said it. He stayed part of the

year at The Armstrong. The rest of the year he flitted around the globe. He hadn't set foot in his home—the castle—since Anna died.

Disappointment was written all over Grace's face. She gestured towards the hamper. 'Why did we need the food? Won't the hotel have food?' Then she gave a little frown. 'And are you sure you'll be able to find somewhere at this time on Christmas Eve when you don't have a reservation?'

There was an edge of panic to her voice. She hadn't wanted to spend Christmas alone—but she didn't want to spend it at the side of a road either.

She could be right. Lots of the hotels in the surrounding area would be full of families in Scotland for Christmas. 'Give me a second,' he said.

He made a quick call, then leaned forward to confer with the pilot. 'Snow is too heavy around that area,' the pilot said quickly. 'The hotel is too remote. Their helipad is notorious for problems.' He shook his head. 'I'd prefer not to, Mr Armstrong.'

Finlay swallowed. He'd used this pilot for years. If he said he'd prefer not to, he was being polite because Grace was here. He glanced at Grace. 'My parents aren't expecting me until Boxing

Day. I don't want to appear early without letting them know.' He pulled a face. 'The hotel I'd thought we could go to has rooms, but—' he nodded to their pilot '—it's remote and our pilot doesn't recommend it.'

Grace's eyes widened. 'So, what do we do, then?'

He sucked in a breath. 'There is somewhere else we could stay.' As he said the words every bit of moisture left his mouth. Part of his brain was in overdrive. Why had he packed the hamper? Had he always known they would end up here?

'Where?' Grace sounded curious.

He hadn't quite met her gaze. He glanced out at the dark night. He had no idea where they were right now. And he had no idea what lay ahead.

Last time he'd been in the castle…

He couldn't even go there. But the practicalities of right now were making him nervous. What would they find at the end of this journey?

After a few years when he'd thought he'd never go back to the castle he'd let his staff go. His mother had made a few casual remarks. He knew that she must have been there. But he also knew that his family respected his wishes.

Grace reached over and touched his arm. Her

warm fingers wrapped around his wrist. 'Finlay, where are you taking me? Where will we be staying?'

'My home,' he said before he changed his mind. 'Drumegan Castle.'

Grace pulled her hand back. 'What?' She looked from one side to the other as if she expected the castle to appear out of thin air. 'You own a castle?' Her mouth was practically hanging open.

It had been a while since he'd spoken about the castle. When they'd first bought it, he'd relished the expression on people's faces when he'd told them he owned a castle. But the joy and love for his property had vanished after Anna's diagnosis and then death.

'You own a castle,' Grace repeated.

He nodded. He had to give her an idea of what might lie ahead. 'I haven't been back there in a while.'

'Why?' As soon as she asked the question, realisation dawned on her and she put her hand up to her mouth. 'Sorry,' she whispered. 'Oh.'

'It's all closed up. I don't even know what it will be like when we get there. It will be cold. I hope the heating still works.' He leaned forward and put his head in his hands. 'Please let the electricity be working.' Then he looked upwards, 'Please let the water be working.' This was beginning to feel like a very bad idea. They might actually be better off at the side of the road than in the castle after five years. 'What am I doing?' He was talking to himself but the words came out loud.

Grace's hand came back. 'Finlay, we don't need to go there if you're not comfortable.' She bit her bottom lip. 'But five years is a long time. Maybe it's time to go back.' Her gaze was steady. 'Maybe it's time to think about whether you want to keep the castle or not.' She squeezed his hand again. 'And maybe it won't be quite as bad if you're not there by yourself.'

He could see the sincerity in her eyes. She meant every word. She wanted to help him. She didn't seem worried about the possibility of no water, no electricity or no heating. Just about every other woman in the world that he'd ever known would be freaking out right now. But Grace was calm. The excitement from the helicopter journey had abated now they'd been travelling for a few hours.

Something washed over him. A sense of relief. His stomach had been in knots. A long time ago he'd loved Drumegan Castle. Loved the approach and seeing the grey castle outline against the sky, towering above the landscape on the top of a hill. It used to give him tingles.

Then, for a while, it had given him dread. That had been the point of staying away for so long. He couldn't imagine coming back here himself. He couldn't imagine opening the front door and being swept away by the wave of emotions.

But even though those things were circulating around his brain, he didn't feel the urge at all to break the connection with Grace's steady brown gaze. There was something about being around her. A calmness. A reassurance he hadn't felt in…so long. He placed his hand over hers. 'I think you could be right.' She was trying so hard to help him, but how much had he done for her?

'You should have told me about your gran,' he said quietly.

She shook her head quickly. 'I couldn't. Once you'd told me about Anna… I just felt so guilty. My grief can't compare with yours. They're two entirely different things.'

She was trying so hard to sound convincing, to stop the tiny waver he could still hear in her voice. Her grief was still raw. His?

He kept holding her hand. 'It's not different, Grace. You lost someone that you loved. This is your first Christmas without that person. I get it.' He gave a rueful smile. 'Believe me, I do.'

He pulled her closer and she rested her head on his shoulder. Next thing he knew the pilot was giving him a shout. 'Five minutes.'

He nudged Grace. 'Wake up, sleepy. We're just about to land.'

She sat up and frowned, rubbing her eyes and looking around. It was still pitch black outside. 'Where on earth are we landing?' she asked.

He smiled. 'At the helipad. The lights are automated.' As he said it they switched on, sending a stream of white light all around them. 'The helipad can be heated to keep it clear. It has its own generator.'

Grace pressed her nose up against the window. 'Is this near the castle? I can't see it.'

She turned and planted one hand on her hip. 'Finlay Armstrong, are you sure you have a castle? It's a caravan, isn't it? You're secretly pranking me and taking me to a forty-year-old caravan with no heating and electricity in the middle of nowhere.'

He raised his eyebrows. 'Don't forget the no water.'

She laughed. 'I couldn't possibly forget that.'

He pulled a face. 'Believe me, once you see the castle, you might prefer a forty-year-old caravan.'

She leaned back with a sigh as they approached the helipad. 'I bet I won't. Stop worrying.'

The helicopter landed smoothly and they jumped out into the biting cold air. 'Whoa!' Grace gave a start. 'I thought London was cold.'

He grabbed her bags. 'I told you to bring layers. Maybe I should have supervised the packing?' He was only half joking. He was curious about where Grace lived and was annoyed he'd been distracted by a business call. It might not have been the most prestigious part of London but he'd have liked to have seen the home she'd shared with her grandmother and had so many good memories of.

He gave a nod to the pilot and walked off to the side as the helicopter took off again. There was a garage next to the helipad and he pressed a button to open the automated door. There was a squeak. And a creek. And finally it rolled upwards revealing a far too smart four-by-four.

Grace turned to face him. 'This is yours?'

'Last time I checked.' He felt up in the rafters of the garage for the keys, fingers crossed it would start. He knew that his father secretly used the car on occasion to 'keep it in running order'. He was just praying it hadn't been too long since he'd last borrowed it.

He put the bags in the boot and Grace climbed in. He waited until he was ready to get in next to her, then flicked another switch—the external lights of the castle.

She let out a gasp. 'What?'

It was almost as if the castle appeared out of nowhere. The white lights illuminating it instantly around the base, the main entrance, the turrets. At the same time more lights came on, picking out the long driveway between the landing pad and castle.

It might have helped that the whole area was covered in a thick layer of snow, making it look even more magical than normal.

Grace turned to face him, her face astounded. '*This* is your castle?'

'What did you expect?'

She pressed herself back against the leather seat as he started the engine. She was transfixed. She lifted up one hand. 'I don't know. I just didn't expect…that. Look at the snow,' she breathed.

He was fighting back the wave of emotions that was threatening to overtake him. The immense sadness was there. But it wasn't because he was grieving for Anna. It was the sudden realisation that he'd truly been away for too long. As soon as the lights had flashed on he'd been struck by how much he'd missed this sight.

Drumegan Castle had always made him so proud. It was every boy's dream to own a castle. According to Anna it had been every girl's dream too. Drumegan might not have been the pink of some Mediterranean castles, or the beige limestone of many English palaces and large houses. Drumegan Castle was built entirely of grey stone, making it look as if it just rose straight up from the green hill on which it was perched. But to him, just the sight of it gave him immense pride. He'd forgotten that.

It seemed he'd forgotten a lot of things.

He started the car and pulled away. 'What do you think?' It was the oddest sensation, but he wanted her approval. Why? He couldn't quite understand. It was important to him that she liked Drumegan Castle as much as he did.

'How many rooms does it have?' She sounded a bit spaced out.

'Rooms or bedrooms?' His reply was automatic. He'd answered so many questions about his home in the beginning he was practically a walking encyclopaedia on Drumegan Castle.

'Either.' She was still just staring at the structure ahead as they moved along the winding driveway.

'Well, it has wings really. Six bedrooms in each wing. Then two main kitchens. A scullery. A ballroom. Five sitting rooms. Three dining rooms. A few studies. And most bedrooms have separate bathrooms. Some of the top rooms have never been renovated. They're still the original servants' quarters.'

'Ah...so *that's* where you're putting me.' Grace had sparked back into life. 'No bed. No bedsheets. No curtains. And probably...' she pulled her hands around her body '...freezing!' She gave an exaggerated shiver.

He tapped the wheel. 'Hold that thought as you pray the heating is still working properly.'

The car moved up the final part of the drive towards the main entrance of the castle. Normally he would sweep around to the back where there were garages. But there didn't seem much point. He didn't expect anyone else to appear and they were both tired.

He pulled up directly outside the main steps and huge traditional carved double doors.

Grace stepped automatically from the car—she didn't need to be told twice. In the bright outside lights she looked pale. And a little nervous. Even though she was wearing the pink winter coat he could see the slight tremor in her body. He walked around to the back of the car and unloaded the cases, the hamper and the cool box. She came over to help and they walked up the flight of steps to the door.

His hand fumbled slightly as he reached for the lock. 'You'll need to give me a second to turn the main alarm off when we get inside. It should only take a few seconds.'

She nodded.

The lock creaked, then rattled as he twisted and jiggled the key. Finally the key turned around. He breathed a sigh of relief as he opened the iron door handle then shouldered the door completely open.

There was a whoosh. A weird kind of noise. Then an incessant little beep. The alarm.

He dumped the bags and walked to the right. The alarm panel was inside the cupboard at the side of the door. It only took a few seconds to key in the code. The light from outside was flooding in. He'd forgotten to mention the glass dome in the main entrance way. It had been put in by the previous owner—an architect and design engineer who obviously had been born before his time. Together with the lights reflecting from outside and the silver twinkling stars above filling the black sky it was a spectacular sight.

The hamper fell with a clatter from Grace's hand as she walked forward under the dome. She held out her hands and spun around as her eyes stayed transfixed above. 'I've never seen anything like it,' she said as she turned slowly.

He smiled as he walked over next to her, moving close. 'It's amazing. It was the first thing I noticed when I came to view the castle.' He pointed above. 'At least I know the electricity is working inside as well as out.'

She gave him a curious stare. 'How do you know that?'

He kept looking upwards. 'Sensors. Think about it—the dome should be covered with snow—just like the rest of outside is. But the engineer who designed it knew that the weight of snow could damage it. He designed one of the first thermal sensors to pick up outside temperatures. The glass is heated—just barely—to stop snow gathering there. I had to have a specialist firm out around ten years ago to update the technology and they could hardly believe it.'

She stopped spinning and stared up at him. She didn't seem to notice how close they were—or she didn't seem to mind. She stared up with her chocolate-brown eyes. 'This place looks amazing. I can't wait to see the rest of it.' She touched his arm. 'Are you okay?'

Still thinking about him. Still showing concern. Anna would have loved Grace Ellis.

'I'm fine. Come on.'

They hadn't even closed the door behind them yet and the bitter winds were sweeping in behind them. He slammed the heavy door shut then walked to another small room to flick a few switches. 'Hot water and boiler should be on. But this place takes a long time to heat up. There are separate heating systems in the different wings so I've just put on the main system and the one for the wing we'll be staying in.'

Did that sound pretentious? He didn't mean it

to. It was a big place, but it could be morning before they finally felt warm here.

He walked over, opening the door to the main sitting room, flicking on the light switch, then stopped in shock.

Grace walked straight into his shoulder.

The artificial light seemed harsh. What greeted them was even harsher. As soon as his foot hit the floor a white mist puffed upwards.

The five windows were shuttered from the inside. The whole room covered in dust sheets. The dust sheets were covered in dust. The dark wooden floor had its own special coating of dust. One curtain was half hanging from a rail. The things that hadn't managed to be covered in dust sheets were coated from head to foot in a thick layer.

Grace gave a huge sneeze. 'Oh, sorry.'

He spun around, sending up a further cloud. 'No. I'm sorry. I didn't realise it would be quite this bad.' He shook his head. 'I just... I just...' The words wouldn't form in his brain.

She reached up and touched his cheek. 'Finlay, it's fine. It's your home. It needs a bit of work.'

'A bit of work? Grace—how on earth can we stay here?'

She folded her arms and looked around. She flicked the edge of a dustsheet and sneezed again as the air clouded. 'It's like that film—you remember—when the spy comes back to the old Scottish mansion house he was brought up in.'

'Remember what happened to that house?'

She let out a laugh. 'Okay, let's go for another film. I could sing the Mary Poppins song as we cleaned up.'

'You honestly want to clean up?' He couldn't quite believe it.

'Why not?' It was quite ironic. There were no airs and graces around Grace Ellis. She took off her coat and started to roll up her sleeves.

She glanced around. 'Let's check out the kitchen. We have some things to put in the fridge.'

Finlay winced. If this was one of the sitting rooms he had no idea what the kitchen would look like.

But he was in for a surprise. The kitchen wasn't dusty at all. Grace ran her fingers along one of the worktops and looked at him in surprise. Then she started opening cupboards, followed by the larder and fridge.

'This place isn't so bad. Someone has kept it clean. Right enough, there isn't a single piece of food in this house. Just as well we brought the hamper.'

Something clicked in his brain. 'My mum. They did offer to look after the place and I said no.' He was almost ashamed to admit that. He walked around. 'But the main hall wasn't so dusty and in here has certainly been emptied and cleaned.' He gave a slow nod. 'All the other rooms have their doors closed. She hasn't gone into them. But the kitchen is open plan. She's only kept things tidy in here.'

Grace gave a nod. 'The surfaces just need a little wipe down.' She walked through a door off to the side then stuck her head back around. 'And there's enough cleaning products through here to clean this whole place a hundred times over.' She went to lift the hamper.

Finlay moved quickly. 'Slow down. Let me.' He picked up the hamper and then the cool box. She swung the door open on the fridge and started emptying the cool box straight into it. 'Why don't you find a cupboard to put some of the things from the hamper? Then we can get started on the main room.'

She was like a whirlwind. He had no idea what time it currently was but Grace seemed to have endless energy. He shook his head. 'I think we should look at the bedrooms.'

Her hands froze midway into the fridge. She dipped back and stared around the door at him. 'What?'

He shook his head and laughed. 'That didn't come out quite the way I meant it to. You must be tired. I'm tired. Let's put the food away, then go to the wing where I turned the heating on. The beds will all be stripped down. I'll need to find the sheets and bedding and make them up.'

She started restocking the fridge and looked amused. 'Do you have any idea where the bedding will be?'

He nodded. 'It's all vacuum-packed so I think it should be okay. I'm just worried the rooms will be as dusty as the sitting room.' He'd said rooms deliberately. He didn't want to make Grace uncomfortable.

Grace closed the fridge door. 'Okay, then, let's go.'

He flicked the lights on as they walked down the corridors. Some cobwebs hung from the light fittings. 'This place feels like the Haunted House at one of the theme parks.'

Grace shivered. He stopped walking. 'I'm sorry, did I scare you? I didn't mean to.'

She looked surprised. 'No, I'm not scared, silly, I'm cold.'

Of course. She'd taken her coat off and left it in the hall. The whole house was still bitterly cold. He opened the first door and gulped. It was every bit as bad as the sitting room. Grace instantly coughed.

'Let's try another,' he said.

So they did. The next room wasn't quite so bad. It only took him a few moments to realise why. He walked over to the fireplace. 'This room has a chimney—a real fire. There's still a chimney sweep who comes in once a year to clear all the chimneys. Between that—and the fact there's still some air circulating means it's not quite so bad.'

He walked over to a cupboard and pulled out some vacuum-packed bedding. Then paused. There was only one king-sized bed in here. He glanced between Grace and the bed. 'We can find another room.'

She raised her eyebrows. 'How many others in this wing have a fireplace?'

Realisation settled over him. 'Only this one.'

She sighed and held up her hands. 'How much energy do you have?' She stuck her hands on her hips. 'This place is still freezing. No one will be taking any clothes off.'

The way she was so matter-of-fact made him laugh out loud. He'd been a bit wary about saying something. He didn't want her to think he'd deliberately brought her up here with something in mind.

His stomach was flipping over and over. This had been his marital home. This room hadn't been the bedroom that he and Anna had shared—that was in another wing. But Grace was the first woman he'd ever brought to this house since Anna had died. All of a sudden he was in a bedroom, in his castle, with another woman, and he wasn't entirely sure how they'd got there.

Grace seemed unperturbed. She walked over to the curtains and gave them a shake. The little cloud of dust circulated around her like fairy dust from a film. She gave a sneeze and grabbed a chair. 'I'm going to take these down and throw them in the washing machine. If they come out okay, we can rehang them tomorrow.' She pointed to the fireplace. 'Why don't you see if you can light the fire? Once I've put these in the wash I'll make up the bed. If I don't get to sleep soon, I'll sleep standing up.'

She was already unhooking the curtains from their pole.

The uneasy feeling drifted away. She made things so easy. Things seemed to make sense around Grace. It was her manner.

He knelt down and checked the fireplace. It was clean and ready to be stocked. He knew exactly where the supplies were. It would only take a few minutes to collect them.

By the time he returned Grace had a smoky outline on her black jumper and jeans from the curtains. 'They're in the wash,' she said happily. 'But I think I'll need to get cleaned up once I've made the bed.'

She shook out the sheets and made up the bed in record time. It was bigger than the average king-size and Finlay tried not to think about how inviting it looked covered with the thick duvet, blankets and masses of pillows.

Grace put a hand on his shoulder as she wheeled her pull-along case behind her. 'You said the hot water would work?'

He nodded.

'Then I'm going to duck in the shower.'

He stood up quickly, brushing his hands. 'As soon as I light the fire I'll go and check out one of the other rooms.'

She shook her head again. 'Honestly, don't worry. I'm pretty sure we can sleep in the giant bed without either of us feeling compromised.' She gave him a smile, 'You've no idea how many layers I can wear.' She opened the door to the bathroom and dragged her case inside. A few seconds later he heard the shower start to run. She stuck her head back outside as he started trying to light the fire. 'But if you decided to go to the kitchen and make some tea I wouldn't object.' She frowned. 'Tea. We did bring tea, didn't we?'

He nodded as the fire sparked into life. 'Tea, milk and biscuits.' He arched his back, stretching out the knots from the long journey. 'Tea I think I can manage.'

Thank goodness he was tired. Thank goodness he was overwhelmed with stepping back inside the castle. If he hadn't been, he would have spent the whole time wondering how on earth he would manage to keep his distance from Grace while they were the only two people here. He shook his head as he headed to the kitchen. He should have thought about this beforehand. If he hadn't been able to resist kissing her under a lamp post in London, how on earth would he keep thoughts of touching her from his head now? He couldn't even think about that bare skin in the shower. No way.

By the time he came back Grace was sitting on the bed, her hair on top of her head, wrapped up in one of the giant duvets. She looked as if she had old-fashioned fleecy pyjamas on. He was pretty sure he was supposed to find them unappealing and unsexy.

Trouble was—he just didn't. Not when they were on Grace. He set the steaming-hot tea down on the bedside table along with some chocolate biscuits. She nodded towards the bathroom. 'I left the shower running for you. Figured you'd want to wash the dust off.' She leaned forward conspiratorially. 'Just don't tell the owner. I hear he keeps tabs on the water usage.'

He put his tea down next to hers. 'I think I can take him,' he said with a smile on his face.

In the dim light of the room all he could focus on was the warmth from her brown eyes. 'We'll see.' She picked up her tea and took a sip. 'Not bad.' She gave an approving nod. 'And just think, Alec didn't even give you written instructions.'

He laughed as he pulled his bag into the bathroom and closed the door behind him. It only took a few seconds to strip off his dusty clothes and step into the warm shower. Grace had left some shampoo and shower gel—both pink, both smelling of strawberries.

He started using them without thinking, let the water stream over his body along with distinctly female scent. His stomach started to flip-flop again.

She'd made things sound so casual. As if sharing a bed was no big deal.

And it wasn't—to most men.

It wasn't as if he hadn't shared a bed with a woman in the last five years. He had—if only for the briefest of moments.

But that hadn't actually been *sharing* a bed. That had been using a bed. Something else entirely. He hadn't slept next to another woman since Anna had died. He hadn't *woken up* with another woman.

That was what made him jittery. That was what was messing with his head.

He couldn't deny the attraction to Grace. His body thrummed around her. He couldn't pretend that it didn't. When he'd kissed her—he'd felt lost. As if time and space had just suspended all around them. His hands rubbed his head harder than they needed to, sending the shampoo over his face and eyes, assaulting his senses with the scent.

He leaned back against the bathroom tiles, adjusting the water to a cooler temperature. The house was still freezing. But the heat in this bathroom seemed ridiculously high. Steam had misted the mirror. It was kind of clawing at his throat, making it difficult to breathe.

He turned the dial on the shower once more; the water turned instantly icy, cooling every part of his body that had dared to think itself too hot. All breath left his body in shock as he turned the knob off.

He grabbed the already semi-wet towel and started drying himself vigorously. He didn't want to think that this was the same towel Grace had used to dry her silky soft skin. He didn't want to think that at all.

He glanced at his still-closed bag. Oh, no. He wasn't a pyjama kind of guy. Never had been. What on earth could he wear in bed with Grace?

He leaned against the other tiled wall and sighed. Boxers. That was all he usually wore.

Maybe he should just stick to that because the room outside was so cold that any part of him that didn't behave might just drop off in the icy temperature. But he wouldn't be comfortable like that around Grace. He had a terrible feeling that in the weird space between almost sleeping and not quite he wouldn't have any control of his thoughts or body reactions. A suit of armour would probably help. Pity the castle didn't have any.

He rummaged through his bag and found a black T-shirt, clean boxers and then, stuck in a zip pocket, a pair of gym shorts. Baggy and mid-thigh-length. He'd obviously planned on visiting the hotel gym on his last trip and not quite managed it. He sent a silent prayer upwards. Thank goodness for being lazy.

He wiped down the mirror with the towel and brushed his teeth as his brain started whirring. What kind of pre-sleep conversation would he have with Grace? What if he snored? What if she snored? He couldn't remember ever feeling this nervous around a woman. It was like being fourteen years old again.

He ran his fingers through his damp hair as he refused to meet his own gaze. He was being ridiculous. He was tired. That was all. That, and being back in the house again, was reviving a whole host of natural memories.

It wasn't quite as hard as he'd thought it would be. Having Grace here certainly helped. Seeing the house so desolate and neglected-looking had been a shock. He'd left it too long. He knew that now.

But now he was here. A thought flicked through his brain. It must be after midnight by now. It must be Christmas Day. At the very least he'd have to wish Grace Merry Christmas and thank her for accompanying him. It was time to stop delaying. Time to realise his duties as a host.

He pulled open the door and was surprised by the warm air that met him. The fire had certainly taken hold. He held his breath.

All he could hear was the comfortable crackle of the fire. And something else.

The noise of deep, soft breaths. Grace was sleeping. Her hair had escaped the knot on top of her head and her dark curls were spread across the white pillowcase. Her pink flannel pyjamas were fastened unevenly, leaving a gap at the base of her pale throat.

She looked exhausted. She looked peaceful.

Turned out he didn't need to worry about pre-sleep conversation at all.

He walked over next to her and picked up his cup of now lukewarm tea. She shifted a little as his shadow fell over her and he froze. His fingers itched to reach out and brush a strand of hair away from her face. But he couldn't. He didn't want to do anything to disturb her. Anything to make her feel uncomfortable.

He walked back around to the other side of the bed, sitting down carefully, cringing as the bed creaked. One quick slug of the tea was enough. He shouldn't have spent quite so long in the shower. He slid his legs under the cool duvet, his skin bristling a little. The pillows were soft, the mattress comfortable under his tired muscles. He pulled the duvet a little higher as he turned on his side to face Grace.

The bed was huge. There was plenty of space between them. There would be no reason to end up on the wrong side of the bed, or touch arms or legs accidentally. He leaned his head on his hand and watched the steady rise and fall of her chest for a few minutes.

Even fast asleep Grace was beautiful. Her lips plump and pink, her pale skin flawless. In the space of a few days she'd woken him up. Woken him up to the world he'd been sleepwalking through these past five years.

Part of him was grateful. Part of him was scared. He didn't know what any of this meant. 'Merry Christmas, Grace,' he whispered as he laid his head on the pillow and went to sleep.

CHAPTER EIGHT

GRACE'S EYES FLICKERED OPEN. It took a few seconds for her to remember where she was. The bed was so comfortable. Her fingers and nose were a little chilled but everything else that was under the covers was cosy.

Her body stiffened. She'd fallen asleep last night while Finlay had been in the shower. She'd tried to stay awake, but as soon as she'd finished her tea and the heat from the fire had started permeating across the room her eyelids had grown so heavy that she couldn't keep them open a second longer.

Her eyes flitted around the room. She'd taken the curtains down last night. She'd need to hang them back up and let them dry. Now the pale light of day was filtering through the windows she could see the pale creams and blue of the room. It was much bigger than a normal bedroom, but the size didn't hide the most important aspect.

It was exquisite. Exactly the type of room you'd

expect in a castle. The bed, tables and furniture were traditional and elegant. Cornicing on the ceiling and a dado rail around the middle of the room, with a glass chandelier hanging in the middle of the room. The two chairs next to the bed were French-style, Louis XVI, ornate with the thick padded seats covered in pale blue patterned fabric. Was it possible the rest of the castle was this beautiful? Between the dim light last night and the clouds of dust she couldn't remember the details of the sitting room.

Now, she was conscious of the heavy breathing next to her. She turned her head just a little, scared to shift in the bed in case she woke him.

Finlay Armstrong's muscular shoulders and arms were above the duvet cover. She had a prime view. All of a sudden her mouth felt oddly dry. He was sleeping. For the first time ever, Finlay looked totally relaxed. There were no lines on his face. None at all. All the usual little stress lines around his forehead and eyes had completely vanished.

He almost looked like a different person. Finlay had always been handsome. But there was always some kind of barrier around him, some protective shield that created tension and pressure. This was the most relaxed she'd ever seen him.

His jaw was shadowed with stubble. Her eyes followed the definition of his forearms and biceps, leading up to his shoulders and muscled chest. He shifted and the duvet moved again. Crumpled next to his shoulder looked like a black T-shirt. Did he have anything else on under these covers?

She squirmed under the bedclothes. Her flannel pyjamas were uncomfortably warm. The heating had obviously kicked in overnight. She slid one foot out of bed then realised she hadn't brought any slippers. The carpet was cool. She'd need to find some socks.

How did she get out of bed without waking him?

Her phone beeped. Except it wasn't really a beep. The jangling continued to echo around the room.

Finlay's eyelids flickered open and he stretched his arms out, one hand brushing her hair.

Her heartbeat flickered against her chest as he turned his head towards her and fixed on her with his sleepy blue eyes. 'Morning,' he whispered.

'Morning,' she replied automatically. She felt

kind of frozen—even though one of her legs was currently dangling out of the bed.

The edges of his lips turned upwards as the phone tune kept going. 'Or should I say Merry Christmas?'

It was like warm melted chocolate spreading over her heart. She'd had so many images in her head about this Christmas—all of them focusing on the fact she'd be alone.

This was the absolute last thing she'd expected to happen. Waking up in bed next to Finlay Armstrong in a castle in Scotland would never have found a way into her wildest imagination. She almost wanted to pinch herself to check she was actually here.

She couldn't help but smile. 'Merry Christmas, Finlay,' she said in a voice that squeaked more than she wanted it to.

He stretched again and pushed the covers back. If she'd been prepared—and if she'd been polite—she wouldn't have been caught staring at his abs and chest muscles as he jumped up in a pair of shorts and reached over for his T-shirt. He slid it easily over his head. Giving her a smile as she watched every movement. 'I take it the heating's kicked in at least. Not as warm as I might have hoped. The fire in here last night made me too warm. We'll need to try and find a happy medium.'

She swung her leg out of bed and stopped dead. She was facing the window—the one she'd removed the dusty curtains from last night. For as far as the eye could see there was thick white snow. It clung to every bump of the terrain. Every tree. Every fence. Every path. She stood up and moved automatically to the window. 'Oh, wow,' was all that came out.

She felt his presence at her shoulder and tried not to think about the fact there wasn't much between her and those taut muscles. 'You wanted snow,' he said quietly.

She nodded. 'Yes. I did.' She turned her head towards him. 'Just how wet are we going to get?'

He raised his eyebrows. 'How wet do you want to get?'

The air was rich with innuendo. She could play this either way. But she couldn't forget how they'd ended up here. She just wasn't sure where she was with Finlay. All she knew was that the more those deep blue eyes looked at her, the more lost she felt.

'It's snow angels all the way,' she said safely.

'But how about we find the Christmas decorations first?'

He nodded. 'Let's get some breakfast. Then, I think I might have a turkey to stick in the oven before we hit the hills. I know where the Christmas decorations are stored—but I've no idea what state they're in.'

Grace shrugged her shoulders. 'No matter. I'd just like to have Christmas decorations up when we eat dinner tonight. We'll need to clean up the sitting room too.'

He hesitated. 'Are you sure? This isn't a busman's holiday, you know. Just because it's the day job, doesn't mean that I expect you to help clean up around here.' He stuck his hands on his hips as he looked at the white view. 'I should probably get a company in.'

Grace shook her head. 'You can do that after Christmas—for the rest of the house. The kitchen is fine. I can rehang the curtains in here, and I'm sure between us we can sort out the other two rooms. It's just a bit of dust.'

It was more than a bit of dust. They both knew that. But Grace was determined to show Finlay that she wasn't a princess. Last night had been a bit of a dream. Ending up at a castle made her seem like a princess. But emotions ran deep.

This was her first Christmas without her grandmother. It was always going to be tough. But Finlay had already made it a bit easier. The change of scenery. The fact that someone had actually thought about her, and considered her, meant a lot.

Today would be hard. Every Christmas aroma would bring back memories of her gran. She'd worked so hard up until now to try and push the reality of today into a place there wasn't time to think about.

Past Christmases with her gran had also been a panacea for something else. It didn't really matter what age you were—being ignored by your mother would always cut deep.

It didn't matter that she'd reached adulthood intact and totally loved by her grandmother. The big gaping hole was always there. She could never escape the fact her mother had all but abandoned her to make a new life for herself. What kind of person did that?

In a way, it had strengthened the bond between her and her grandmother. Both of them trying to replace what the other had lost. But it also made it hard for her to form new relationships with other people. Grace struggled to make friends easily, because she struggled to trust. The girls from Maids in Chelsea were the closest friends she'd ever made. As for men? It was easy to blame her gran's illness and juggling jobs to explain why she'd never had a truly lasting relationship. She could just say it was down to poor taste in men. But the truth was, she'd always found it hard to trust anyone, to believe that someone would love her enough not to abandon her. It was easier to keep her feelings cocooned. At least then they were safe.

But now? Her biggest problem was that every second she was around Finlay she became a little bit more attached. Saw another side of him that she liked, that she admired, that she might even love a little. But he was her boss. They lived completely different lives. Her heart didn't even know where to start with feelings like these.

So why had they ended up here together?

Finlay's fingers intertwined with hers as they looked at the snow together. The buzz was instant, straight up her arm to her heart. There was so much she could say right now. So many tumbling thoughts.

'Let's get dressed,' said Finlay as he turned and walked away.

Grace folded her arms and smiled out at the untouched snow. This Christmas was shaping up to be completely different from what she'd ever imagined.

Her phone beeped and she pulled it from her bag. Sophie.

Where are you? I dropped by the flat.

Grace pressed buttons quickly, knowing exactly the response she'd get.

With my boss. In Scotland.

She smiled, added a quick, See you all at the Snowflake Ball, and tucked the phone into her bag, knowing it would probably buzz for the rest of the day.

It was like having someone with boundless energy next to you all day. Grace didn't seem to know how to sit down. Five minutes at breakfast was her record. After that, she'd rehung the curtains, then started to power around the dining room.

Meanwhile he'd been in the place he clearly wasn't destined for.

Finlay frowned at the instructions. They must have got a little wet in his pocket. They were a bit smudged. He'd found a suitable tray for the turkey and followed Alec's instructions. But this basting thing looked complicated. Would he even get to leave the kitchen at all today?

Grace appeared with a smudge on her nose, laughing, watching him squint at the instructions. 'How's the turkey?' She smiled with a hand on her hip.

He shook his head. It was too, too tempting. His thumb was up wiping the smudge from her nose instantly, the rest of his hand touching the bottom of her chin.

Whatever she'd opened her mouth to say next had been lost. She just stared at him with those big brown eyes. For a second, he couldn't breathe. He couldn't inhale.

Every thought in his head was about kissing her. Tasting those lips. Running his fingers through her soft hair, tied back with a pink ribbon. She'd changed into a soft pink knit jumper and blue figure-hugging jeans. Her face was make-up-free, but, although she was as beautiful as ever, today she looked different. She looked happy. She was relaxed.

He could almost sense a peaceful aura buzzing around her. His stomach turned over. He'd done the right thing. He'd done the right thing bringing Grace here—both for him, and for her.

It was as if she was caught in the same glow that he was. 'How's your Christmas going?' she whispered.

He couldn't tear his gaze away. 'Better than I could have hoped for.'

She put a hand over his at the side of the turkey tray. 'Then let's get this old girl in the oven. I've found the Christmas decorations, but I couldn't find the tree.'

'Oh.'

Her hand was still on his. 'What do you mean, oh?'

He picked up the tray—this turkey was heavier than it looked—and slid the tray into the oven. He picked up the other items that Alec had given them, onion, stuffing and chipolatas, and pushed them back in the fridge. 'We can put them in later.'

He closed the oven door with a bang and checked the temperature. Grace folded her arms and leaned against the countertop. Finlay looked around the room for his navy jumper. It only took a moment to find it and pull it on. He glanced at Grace's feet. 'Do you have other boots?'

'Why?'

He walked around her and held the door to the main hall open. 'Because I don't have an artificial tree. I've never used one at Drumegan Castle.' He gestured with his hand. 'I've got a whole wood out there full of pine trees. All we need to do is go and get one.'

Her eyes widened. Even from this far he could see the enthusiasm. 'Really, you're going to cut down a real Christmas tree?'

He nodded. 'Snow angels, anyone?'

Her eyes sparkled. 'I'll race you!'

In the end she hadn't worn the very expensive pink winter coat that Finlay had bought her. He'd found old waterproof jackets in the cupboard and they'd worn them on their hike across the grounds, complete with wheelbarrow and electric saw.

'I'm kind of disappointed,' she teased as he wheeled it towards the wood.

'Why?' He looked surprised.

Her feet were heavy in the snow. It really was deep here. Finlay hadn't been kidding. She gave him a teasing smile. 'I kind of hoped you'd just stomp over here with an axe, cut down the tree then throw it over your shoulder and bring it back to the castle.'

He let out a laugh. 'Really? Just like that?' He stopped wheeling, obviously trying to catch his breath just at the edge of the wood. 'Well, I guess I could do that if you want.' He pointed to a tiny tree just at the front of the wood. It was about two feet tall. 'But this would be our Christmas tree. What do you think?'

She sidled up next to him. It had started to snow again and the snow was collecting on her shoulders with a few flakes on her cheeks. 'Finlay Armstrong, you know how much I love Christmas, don't you?'

She'd tilted her chin towards him. All he had to do was bend down a little.

He couldn't help the smile that automatically appeared. Grace's enthusiasm was infectious. 'Grace Ellis, I might have noticed that about you.'

'You did?' She blinked, snowflakes landing on her thick lashes.

His hand naturally went around her waist,

pulling her closer. Her hands slid up the front of his chest. 'I might have. So, I want you to look around the wood and find your perfect Christmas tree. When you find it, it's all yours.'

She was watching him carefully. 'All mine, I like the sound of that.'

He licked his lips. A few weeks ago, if someone had told him he'd be standing in the castle grounds on Christmas Day, waiting to cut down a tree with a beautiful woman in his arms, he would have thought they were crazy.

That would never, ever happen for him again.

And yet...he was here. With Grace. And for the first time in years he actually felt happy. He wasn't imagining this. This was real. There was a real connection between them.

She gave her hand a little thump against his chest and looked upwards. 'Snow's getting heavier.' She winked at him. 'It must have heard I was here. Snow angels waiting. Let's find this tree, Finlay. We have a date in the snow.'

A date in the snow.

He knew exactly what she meant and the words were casual. A date. Hadn't they already had a few dates? Had he been dating without really knowing it?

She walked ahead and gave a shout a few minutes later. Then she gave a squeal. He darted through the trees. She was jumping up and down, clapping her hands together. 'This is it. This is the tree. It's perfect. Don't you think? It will look gorgeous in the sitting room.'

She was infectious, truly infectious. She was right. She'd picked a perfect tree. Immaculately shaped, even branches and just the right height. 'It's not quite perfect,' he said as he stepped forward.

'It's not?' She leaned back a little, looking up as if she was trying to spot the flaw.

'No,' he said as he reached the tree and stretched his hand through the branches to catch hold of the trunk. 'Too much snow.'

He started shaking the tree as she screamed, covering them both in the tumble of snow from the branches. It fell thick and fast, sliding down his neck and making him shiver.

Grace fell backwards with a shriek, laughing as she fell.

She lay there for a few seconds, trying to catch her breath. He pulled his hand back and stepped over her. 'Okay down there?'

She was lying looking up at the sky. 'No,' she

said firmly. 'I've been hoodwinked by a crazy Scots man.' She held her hand up towards him.

He grabbed it, steeling himself to pull her upwards. But Grace was too quick for him. She gave him an almighty wrench, yanking him downwards to her and the heavy snow.

He landed with a splat, face first in the snow next to her, only part of his body on hers.

Her deep, throaty laugh echoed through the wood. Once she started, she couldn't stop.

He sucked in a breath and instead sucked in a mouthful of snow, making him snort and choke. He tried to get up on his knees to clear his mouth, but Grace grabbed hold of his arm. 'Oh, no, you don't.' She was still laughing.

He spluttered again, this time getting rid of snow and starting to laugh himself. She'd got him. She'd got him good.

'You promised me something,' she said.

The laughing had stopped and she sounded deadly serious. He lay down next to her in the snow. 'Okay, then. What did I promise?'

She reached over and touched the side of his cheek. It was the tenderest of touches. 'You promised me snow angels,' she whispered. 'And I plan on collecting.'

He only had to move forward a couple of inches. Maybe she was talking about snow angels. But the heat between them had been rising all day; it was a wonder they hadn't melted all the snow around them.

He captured her sweet lips in his. Her cheeks were cold. The hat she'd pulled from her pocket earlier had landed on the snow, letting her hair fan out in the snow—just as it had on the pillow last night. That memory sparked a rush of blood around his body.

He pulled his hand from his gloves and tangled it through her hair. Her other hand caught around the back of his neck, melding her body next to his. It didn't matter that the ground was freezing and snow was getting in places it just shouldn't. He didn't care about anything other than the connection to this woman.

Somewhere deep inside him a little spark was smouldering. Willing itself to burn brighter and harder.

Grace responded to every movement, every touch, matching him step by step. He didn't have any doubt the feelings were mutual. He was surprised when she slowly pulled back and put one arm against his chest. She was smiling though.

'Parts of me I didn't know could get wet, are wet.' She sighed. 'I guess this would be the right time to collect on the snow angels.'

He laughed and nodded. Kissing lying in the snow wasn't an ideal arrangement. He knew that. He just didn't care about the wet clothes.

He looked over at the piece of ground a little away from the trees. 'To make snow angels, we need to do it where there are no other marks. Let's go over there.'

He took her arm and pulled her up. They'd only walked a few steps when she stopped dead. 'Look!'

'What?' He looked around near the trees and bush she was pointing to.

'Holly,' breathed Grace. 'It's holly.'

She was right; the jaggy green leaves and red berries were poking out from underneath the snow. She grabbed hold of his arm. 'Can you cut some? Wouldn't it be gorgeous to have some fresh holly in the house?'

There it was again. That infectious enthusiasm. If she could bottle it and sell it she could be a millionaire. He put his arm around her waist. 'Snow angels first, then the tree, then the holly. You could freeze out here.'

She nodded and shivered. 'I think I already am.'

He took her hand and led her across the snow, turning around to face the castle. 'How about here?'

She nodded as she looked at their trail of footprints in the snow.

'Then let's do it.' Finlay grinned as he held out his arms and fell backwards in the snow, landing with a thud. *'Oof!'*

Grace looked a bit shocked, then joined in, turning to face the castle, holding out her arms and falling backwards. Her thud wasn't nearly as loud.

They lay there for a few seconds. The clear blue sky above them, the white-covered world all around them, with the majestic grey castle standing like a master of all it surveyed.

'It's just beautiful here,' breathed Grace.

Finlay wasn't thinking about the cold. His eyes were running over the hundreds of years old building he'd neglected for the last five years. It had stood the test of time, again and again. It had been here before him. And it would still be standing long after he had gone. 'Yes, yes, it is,' he agreed.

Pieces were starting to fall into place for him.

The brickwork at one of the turrets looked as if it needed work. There were a few misaligned tiles on one part of the roof—probably the result of one of Scotland's storms. All things that could be easily mended.

The cold was soaking in through his jacket and jeans. All things could be mended. It just depended on whether you were willing to do the repairs.

'Hey? Are you going?'

He smiled again. Grace was the best leveller in the world. 'Yes, let's go.'

They yelled and shouted as they moved their arms up and down in the heavy snow. Grace started singing Christmas songs at the top of her voice.

He hadn't felt this happy in such a long time. He hadn't felt this free in such a long time. He turned his head and watched her singing to the sky with a huge smile on her face—this was all because of Grace. He just couldn't deny it.

When she finally stopped singing they lay in the snow for a few seconds.

'Thanks, Grace.'

She looked surprised. 'For what?'

He held up one damp arm. 'For this. For helping me come back here. For making something that should be hard feel as if I was meant to do it. I was meant to be here.'

She rolled over in the snow onto her stomach, facing him. 'That's because I think you were, Finlay. Maybe it was just time.'

He nodded in agreement. 'Maybe it was.'

She pushed herself up onto her knees. 'Thank you too.'

'What for?'

She smiled. 'For making a Christmas that I thought I was going to hate, into something else entirely. Snow? A castle? What more could a girl ask for?' She shook some snow off her jacket. 'Except pneumonia, of course.'

He pushed himself up. 'You're right. Let's go. The tree will only take a few minutes to cut down and we can grab some holly along the way.'

From the second they'd got back in the castle and showered and changed, things had seemed different. This time, Grace had put on the only dress she'd brought. It was black with a few sparkles. She'd always liked dressing up on Christmas Day and she was hoping Finlay would appreciate the effort. There hadn't been time to do anything but dry her hair so she left it in waves tied back with the same pink ribbon as earlier. Finlay was in the kitchen, muttering under his breath as he basted the turkey—again.

She nudged him as she watched. 'What do you say we make this easy?'

'How?'

'That tray of roast potatoes, stuffing and chipolatas? Just throw them in next to the turkey.'

'You think that will work?'

She shrugged. 'Why not? Let's put the Christmas pudding on to steam. We might as well. We have a tree to decorate.'

Something flashed behind his eyes. She wasn't sure what, because it disappeared almost as soon as it appeared. He nodded. 'Yes, we do, don't we? Okay, then.' He threw the rest of the food into the turkey tray. 'At least if nothing else works, we still have the soup. It's stored in the fridge. At least it's safe.'

Grace put a pan of water on to boil and arranged the steamer on top with the small muslin-wrapped Christmas puddings. 'All done.'

She'd left the cardboard boxes full of decorations in the sitting room. Finlay had already arranged the Christmas tree on the stand—just waiting to be decorated—and lit the fire to try and warm the room some more.

As they walked through to the room together she could sense something about Finlay. A reluctance. A worry.

The aromas around her were stirring up a whole host of memories. She was so used to making Christmas dinner with her grandmother. While the Christmas pudding was steaming they normally dug out some old board games and played them together.

It was hard not to have her around. It was hard to face the first Christmas without her. Her hand went automatically to her eyes and brushed a tear away. She wanted to enjoy this Christmas. She wanted to know that she could still love her favourite time of year without the person she usually spent it with.

What scared her most was how much she was beginning to feel about the man she was secluded with in this castle. That one kiss had stirred up so many hidden emotions inside her. Apart from a dusty castle, there were no other distractions here.

It was just him. And her.

It was difficult to ignore how he made her feel.

It was difficult to fight against a build-up of emotions in an enclosed space.

She rummaged through the box and heard a little tinkle of bells. It reminded her of an old film she'd watched with her grandmother. She looked upwards and smiled. It didn't make her feel sad; instead a little warmth spread through her. 'Love you, Gran,' she murmured.

She pulled a strand of tinsel from one of the boxes, bright pink, and wrapped it around her neck. Then, she flicked the switch on the radio. The words of *Let it Snow* filled the room..

She turned to face him and held up her hands. 'Think they knew where we were?'

'Could be.' His voice seemed a little more serious than before; his eyes were fixed on the cardboard boxes.

She moved over next to him and put her hands on his chest. He'd changed into a long-sleeved black shirt, open at the neck, and well-cut black trousers. It would be easy to spend most of the day staring at his muscular thighs and tight backside. 'We don't have to do this, Finlay.'

He shook his head. 'No, we do. *I* do.' She stood back and let him open the flaps of the first box and start lifting out the decorations.

They were all delicately wrapped in tissue paper. He unwrapped one after the other. She could see the expression on his face. Each one brought back a different memory. She put her hand over his. 'If I was at home right now, I'd be feeling exactly the same way,' she said reassuringly. 'Some of the decorations my gran and I have had for years. Some of them we made together. There were several I just couldn't hang this year. I get it. I do.'

His grateful blue eyes met hers. There was pain in them, but there was something else too. A glimpse of relief.

His hands seemed steady as he handed each one to her to hang. Occasionally he gave a little nod. 'That one was from Germany. This one from New York.'

Her stomach twisted a little. She felt like Scrooge being visited by the ghost of Christmas past. All of these memories were wrapped around Anna. She didn't expect him to forget about his dead wife. But she needed to be sure that when he kissed her, when he touched her, he wasn't thinking of someone else. She wasn't a replacement. She wouldn't ever want to be. Lots of his actions made her think he was ready to move on. But this, this was eating him up. Her stomach flipped over. She'd brought something, lifted something on instinct in the penthouse in London. Maybe it hadn't been such a good idea after all.

She looked in the box and gave him a smile. 'Hey, I haven't found anything purple yet. Isn't there anything that will match our decorations down in London?'

He gave her a smile and shook his head. 'There's nothing in those boxes. But I did think about purple before we left. Give me a second.'

His footsteps echoed down the hall and she looked around. The fire was flickering merrily, giving off a distinctive heat. The smell of the turkey and Christmas pudding was drifting across the main hall towards them. Between that, and the Christmas tree, this place really did have the aroma and feel of Christmas.

Finlay came back holding a string of Christmas lights—the same ones they'd used in the hotel. Grace gasped. 'You brought purple lights?'

He nodded. 'I don't even know. I didn't think I'd planned to come here. But I know the lights we used to have here don't work any more. I liked the purple lights from the hotel so I brought some along.'

He started to wind them around the tree. It was almost finished. The lights should have gone on first, but Finlay managed to wrap them around the tinsel and hanging decorations without any problem. When he'd finished he flicked the switch to light up the room.

It had grown steadily darker outside, now the room was only lit with the orange crackling fire and the purple glowing lights. Together with the smells of Christmas it was almost as if some Christmas spirit had been breathed back into Drumegan Castle.

Grace felt her heart flutter. There was one last thing she had to do. She was doing it for the right reasons. Even if she did have a tiny bit of selfishness there too. She needed to know where Finlay was. She needed to know how ready he was.

'I brought something too. Give me a minute.'

She practically ran along the hall, finding the white tissue paper and bringing the item back. Finlay was standing looking around the room. She couldn't quite read the expression on his face.

So, she took a deep breath and held out the item with a trembling hand.

It was now, or never. Time to find out what the future might hold.

* * *

Finlay's breath was caught somewhere in his throat. He didn't need to unwrap the item to know what it was.

Grace's hand was shaking. He could see that. He reached up and put his hand under hers, taking his other hand to pull back the delicate tissue paper.

'You brought this?'

She nodded. It wasn't just her hand that was shaking. Her voice was too. 'I thought it might be important. I thought it might be important for you.'

He pulled back the tissue paper on the white ceramic Christmas angel. This time when he looked at it, he didn't feel despair and angst. He didn't feel anger and regret. He looked into the eyes of the woman that was holding it. It was almost as if she were holding her heart in her hand right now.

He knew exactly how she felt.

Grace had brought this. Even though she'd been feeling lonely and sad this Christmas she'd still thought of him.

He could see how vulnerable she was right now. It was written all over her face. He reached up and touched her cheek. A sense of peace washed over him.

Anna. She was here with him. He could almost feel her smiling down on him. It was as if a little part of him unravelled. Anna had made him promise he'd move on. He'd find love again.

He'd locked that memory away because he'd never imagined it possible.

But he'd never imagined Grace.

Did she know how gorgeous she looked in that black dress that hugged her curves and skimmed out around her hips?

He lifted the white ceramic angel and clasped Grace's hand as they walked over to the tree together. As he lifted the angel to hang it from the top of the tree there was the sound of fireworks outside. Bright, colourful, sparkling fireworks lighting up the dark Christmas night sky.

Everything about this just felt right. He reached up and gave the pink ribbon holding Grace's hair back a little tug. As it came away in his hand he rearranged her hair, letting the loose curls tumble all around her face. 'You always tie it back. I like it best like this,' he said. 'While you're in the snow, and while you're lying in bed.'

Grace's eyes were glistening. This time when

she smiled the warmth reached all the way into her brown eyes. Her sadness was gone. Banished. 'We haven't sorted out our sleeping arrangements for tonight,' she said huskily. 'I think we forgot to clean the other bedroom.'

He pulled her closer. 'I think we did. But I've got another idea.'

She tilted her chin up towards him. 'What is it?'

He nodded towards the fire and rug in front of it. 'I was thinking of a picnic. A Christmas picnic with a mishmash of turkey, stuffing, potatoes, chipolatas and Christmas pudding, all in front of our real fire.'

She licked her bottom lip. 'Sounds good to me. In fact, it sounds perfect. Do we have any wine? Or any champagne?'

He lowered his head, his lips brushing against the soft delicate skin at the bottom of her neck. 'I think we might have brought some with us.'

She laughed, her fingers reaching for his chin and bringing it up next to hers. She met his lips with hers. 'How about you grab the food and champagne and I grab us a blanket?'

He didn't want to let her out of his grasp. Not

when he could feel all her curves against his. 'How quick can you be?'

She winked. 'Quicker than you. Just grab an oven glove and bring the whole tray and some knives and forks.' She stood on her tiptoes and whispered in his ear. 'Last one back pays a forfeit.'

'What will that be?'

She raised her eyebrows as she walked backwards to the door. 'You'll find out, slowcoach.'

He loved that she was teasing him. He'd already decided she could win. 'Oh, and, Grace?'

She spun around at the door. 'Yes?'

He winked at her as his mind went directly to other places. 'Forget the flannel pyjamas. You won't be needing them.'

CHAPTER NINE

THIS TIME WHEN she woke up in the castle, underneath was hard and uncomfortable. The arms around her were warm and reassuring, as was the feel of Finlay at her back. His soft breathing against her neck and feel of his heartbeat against her shoulder sent waves of heat throughout her body.

She couldn't help the soft little moan that escaped her lips. Neither could Finlay; she smiled as she recognised the instantaneous effect it had on him too.

'How do you feel about a Boxing Day excursion?' he murmured in her ear.

She leaned back further into him, relishing the bare skin against hers. 'What do you mean?'

He cleared his throat. 'I'd told my mum, dad and sister I would visit today, remember? How do feel about coming along?'

She turned onto her back so she could face him. 'You want me to meet your mum and dad?'

The tiny hairs on her arms stood on end. Last night had been magical. Last night had felt like a dream. She'd never, ever experienced a connection like that. For Grace, it had felt like coming home to the place she'd always meant to be.

Nothing had ever seemed as right to her. But she was worried about what it meant to Finlay. His inviting her to meet his mum and dad today was sending a million reassuring *go faster* signals through her body.

She snaked her arms around his neck. 'I'd love to meet your mum and dad. And your sister. Do you think they'll be okay about meeting me?'

He gave a gentle laugh. 'Oh, I think my mum will measure you for a pair of family slippers.' He dropped a kiss on her lips. 'Don't worry, my family will love you.'

It was easy to respond to his kisses. Even though her brain was focusing on the family-loving-her part. Everything about this Christmas was turning out to be perfect.

The expression on his mother's face when she opened the door was priceless. She flung her arms around his neck while the whole time she stared at Grace.

'This is Grace,' he said quickly as he slid his hand into hers for reassurance. 'We met at work and she came up for Christmas at the castle with me.'

His mother's chin bounced off the floor. 'Fraser!' she shouted at the top of her voice. 'Aileen!' He imagined his father pushing himself out of his chair at the pitch of his mum's voice. 'You spent yesterday at the castle? Why? You could have come here.'

He glanced at Grace and gave her a smile. Yesterday had been better than he could ever have imagined. Nothing could have matched that. He edged around his mother, who was still standing in the doorway in shock. 'You knew I was coming today. That seemed enough.'

His father walked through from the living room and only took a few seconds to hide his shock. He greeted Finlay, then Grace with a huge bear hug. He wasn't even discreet about the whisper in Grace's ear. 'Watch out for Aileen, she's pregnant, cranky and will ask a million questions.'

For Grace it was a wonderful day. The love between the family members was clear. It reminded her of the relationship she'd shared with her grandmother. Aileen didn't hide in the least the fact she was quizzing Grace. But it was all good-natured.

The family shot occasional glances between each other. But all of them were of warmth, of relief. It was obvious they were delighted that Finlay had brought someone to meet them. They obviously wanted him to be happy. Anna was mentioned on occasion. But it wasn't like a trip down memory lane. It was only ever in passing, in an occasional sentence. And she was glad; she didn't want them to tiptoe around her. Not if there was any chance that this relationship could go somewhere.

The board games were fiercely competitive. She paired up with Finlay's dad and managed to trounce him on more than one occasion. When it got late, Finlay's mum, Fran, gave her a little nod, gesturing her through to the kitchen where she was making a pot of tea. 'I've made up Finlay's room for you both. No need to go back to the castle. We usually drink tea, then move on to wine or port and some Christmas cake.'

Grace smiled. She liked the way Fran said it. It was like a warm welcome blanket. Letting her know she was welcome to stay, as well as introducing their family traditions. She picked up the tray with the teapot and cups. 'Thanks, Fran, will I just take these through?'

Fran picked up the port bottle and tray with Christmas and Madeira cake and gave Grace a nudge. 'Let's go.'

Finlay met her at the door; he opened his mouth to speak but his mother cut him off.

'I was just letting Grace know the sleeping arrangements. Now, we're going to have a drink.' She raised her eyebrows at Finlay. 'I believe there was some cheating going on at that last game. I mean to get my revenge.'

Finlay slung his arm around Grace's shoulder. 'Are you okay with this?'

She knocked him with her hip as she smiled back. 'Oh, I'm fine. I mean to defend my winner's crown by all means necessary.' She leaned forward and laughed. 'Brace yourself, Mr Armstrong. You haven't even seen my winning streak yet.'

Firsts. These last few days had been full of them.

It woke him in the middle of the night.

First time since Anna had died that he'd allowed the hotel to be decorated. First time he'd brought someone else to the castle. First time he'd kissed another woman and actually *felt* something. First time he'd introduced his family to someone. First time in five years he'd actually enjoyed a Christmas instead of working straight through.

First time he'd woken up in his mother's house with someone who wasn't his wife.

What was completely obvious was how much his family had relished having Grace there. He could almost see the relief flooding from his mum and dad that he might actually have met someone, and he might actually be ready to move on.

He could hear her steady breathing next to him. But instead of feeling soothed, instead of wanting to embrace the idea of listening to this time after time, he felt an undeniable wave of panic.

They headed back to London today. Reality was hitting. How on earth would things be when they got back to the real world?

He worked goodness knew how many hours a week. He spent most months ping-ponging around the world between various hotels. There was no way he had time for a relationship.

It was as if a cold breeze swept over his skin.

Guilt was creeping in around the edges of his brain. He'd brought another woman to Drumegan Castle and slept with her there. He'd let Grace decorate, feel at home, help clean up and make snow angels in the ground. Most of the time he'd spent with Grace at Drumegan he'd enjoyed. He'd only thought of Anna in fleeting moments. And Grace had been the biggest instigator of that when she'd brought out the ceramic angel. His last physical link to Anna.

The woman that he should have been thinking of. Not Grace.

He shivered as her warm eyes flickered open next to him. 'Morning.' Her sexy smile sent pulses through his body and he pushed the duvet back and stood up quickly.

'Morning. I've got some work to do. Some business calls to make. I might be a few hours. I'm sure my mum will fix you some breakfast.' He was slipping on his jeans and pulling a T-shirt over his head as he spoke. Grace sat upright in the bed, her mussed-up hair all around her face. She looked confused—and a little hurt. 'Oh, okay. No problem. I'm sure I can sort myself out.'

There was no excuse. None. But he couldn't

help it. His head was so mixed up he just needed some space.

And that was easy. Under the fake guise of work his mum, dad and sister were delighted to entertain Grace for the next few hours. Right up until they were ready to head back to the helipad at the castle.

His mother's bear hug nearly crushed him. 'It's been so good to see you, honey. She's fabulous. I love her. Bring her back soon.'

His hand gripped the steering wheel the whole way back to Drumegan Castle's helipad. All of a sudden he didn't feel ready for this. It seemed rushed. It had come out of nowhere. Could he really trust his feelings right now, when he'd spent the last five years shut off?

He couldn't help the way he was withdrawing. It seemed like the right thing to do.

'I think I should be honest, Grace. The past few days have been wonderful. But up here—in Scotland, staying in the castle—this isn't the real world. I'm sorry. I think I made a mistake asking you up here. I knew how you were feeling about Christmas, and I was dreading coming up here again, and I think I might have given you the wrong idea. I'm just not ready for another relationship. Not yet, anyway. I'm not going to be able to give you what you want, Grace, or what you deserve. You should have a partner who loves only you, who wants to settle down and can commit time and energy to your family. I'm sorry, but I'm just not that person.'

She'd stopped noticing the whirring of the helicopter blades. All she could hear right now was the quiet voice next to her. It was almost as if he was speaking in hushed tones so she'd have to lean closer to hear. But the truth was, these were words she'd never wanted to hear.

This morning had been awkward. This afternoon had been worse. She'd almost been relieved when they'd said their goodbyes to Finlay's lovely family and driven back to the helipad at the castle.

She hadn't been able to ask Finlay why he was on edge. And now that made her angry. She'd been close enough to get naked and make love to him, but she didn't feel secure enough to ask what was wrong. Now, after giving her a Christmas she could only have dreamed of, he was unceremoniously dumping her. And he wasn't even doing it that well. He might have waited until they'd landed at The Armstrong. At least then she could have walked straight down the stairs and into the bar.

She tried to push all the angry thoughts aside. Finlay looked terrible. He was pale and his hands were constantly twitching on his lap. He wasn't the cool, remote man she'd first met. But he wasn't the dashing businessman either. Who was it she'd actually fallen in love with?

Her heart stuttered. That was it. That was why those few words felt as if they were wrenching her stomach inside out. Slowly but surely over the last few days Finlay Armstrong had stolen piece after piece of her heart. From that first moment on the roof of The Armstrong, from that tiny stroke of her cheek. From the shopping trip for the decorations, the drinks at the staff party and that first kiss under the lamppost.

He'd recognised her aching and lonely soul and embraced it. She'd given him space. She'd understood visiting Drumegan Castle was hard. But she'd felt as if they'd stood shoulder to shoulder the whole way. When they'd made love on Christmas Day, and he'd taken her to meet his family on Boxing Day, everything had just seemed to be surrounded in pink clouds.

But the storm had swept in. Why? What on earth had she done wrong?

She nervously licked her lips. The last few days had given her something else. A confidence she'd never felt before. She'd had a glimmer of a job that she might love. She'd found something she enjoyed and could be good at. It was a path she wanted to explore.

But she'd wanted Finlay to walk that path alongside her.

She lifted her chin and looked at him. Losing her gran had taught her one thing: love was worth reaching for and holding onto. She deserved love. She deserved to find happiness. She couldn't accept anything less.

It was so hard not to reach for his hand. She took a deep breath. 'I understand this Christmas has been hard, Finlay—I do. I understand that visiting the castle took courage. And it must have whipped up a whole host of memories that maybe you'd forgotten. But I have to ask you this.' She met his gaze, even though it killed her to do so. 'It's been five years, Finlay. Five years that you've turned your back on love. How much longer will it take? Do you think you'll ever be ready to love someone again?'

He could barely meet her gaze. 'It's been an amazing few days, Grace, but no, I'm not looking for love again. I don't think I'll ever be ready.'

She breathed in slowly through her nose. She wanted to shout. She wanted to cry. She wanted to punch him right in the chest. Hadn't he looked at Drumegan Castle and said he'd left things far too long? Hadn't he said that in a few different ways to her?

She'd obviously misunderstood—and that was her own foolish fault. When he'd talked about the neglected castle she'd assumed there was some parallel to himself and his life.

But that was clearly all in her head.

Finlay Armstrong might be the most handsome man she'd ever met. He might be the only man she'd ever felt a connection like this with. He might be the only man who'd stamped all over her fragile heart.

She could almost hear her gran's voice in her ears. She straightened her shoulders and looked him straight in the eye. He'd been right. She deserved so much better than he could offer. She loved him completely, with her whole entire heart. The one that was currently shattered all around them. She had too much pride for this.

She wasn't going to hang around waiting for any scrap of his attention when she was worthy of so much more.

She bit her lips as tears threatened to pool in her eyes.

No. She wouldn't let them. He wouldn't see her cry. He wouldn't know just how much this hurt.

She kept her voice steady. 'Then thank you for a nice Christmas, Finlay. But now we're on our way home—it's clearly best that we both resume our own lives.'

CHAPTER TEN

HE FELT WRETCHED. It was as if a huge cloud of misery had descended over his head in an air of permanence.

He'd been miserable before. He could buy the T-shirt and wear it. But this was different.

He hadn't lost his wife. That was an understandable misery.

This time, he'd lost Grace. The strong, proud woman he still saw walking about his hotel on a daily basis. She didn't look in his direction—not once. She didn't try and engage in conversation. His few 'good mornings' had been resolutely ignored.

But that wasn't the thing that made him feel wretched.

It was the fact that when she thought no one was watching, her shoulders would slump, her head would bow and she'd pull a tissue from her apron.

Grace. The girl with the sparkling eyes, gorgeous smile and biggest heart in the world.

He'd done this.

This morning he'd woken up and turned over in bed. The empty space beside him hadn't just felt empty—it had felt like a massive void.

He'd never considered himself a coward. But why had he retreated so quickly? Was he actually scared? He hated feeling like this. And he hated the way he'd made Grace feel.

The sunlight sparkled off something in the corner of the room. Silver paper. The gift that Mrs Archer had left him. He'd forgotten to open it.

He stood up and walked over. It took a few minutes to unfurl the curling silver ribbons and unwrap the silver paper. Inside was a black box. He flipped it open. An engraved silver heart gleamed at him.

Memories are special in every single way,
But new memories can be made every single
day.

A long red ribbon was attached at the top. It was a Christmas decoration. Ready to be hung on a tree.

Right alongside his ceramic angel.

* * *

There was noise outside her flat as she approached. Grace froze. The last thing she needed was trouble. All she wanted to do was get inside, pull on her pyjamas and make some toast.

As she took another step forward she recognised the voices. She straightened up and walked around the corner. 'Emma, Sophie, Ashleigh— what are you doing here?'

'Grace!' Their shouts were probably heard all up and down the stairwells of the flats. She found herself enveloped in a group hug. Tears prickled at her eyes.

'You missed Christmas with us.' Emma held up a bag that clinked.

Ashleigh held up another, her engagement ring gleaming in the dim hall lights. 'Let us in, we want to hear all your news.'

Sophie was clutching a huge trifle in a glass bowl. 'What happened with your boss?'

She couldn't hold it together a second longer. She'd tried so hard all day. Seeing Finlay at the hotel was torture. Because now she knew what they could share together, she was having trouble being anything but angry.

She dissolved into tears of frustration.

'Grace? Grace? What's wrong?'

The keys were fumbled from her hands, her door opened and she was ushered into the flat. Within two minutes glasses appeared, wine was poured and her jacket was pulled from her shoulders. She sank down onto the sofa as Ashleigh opened the biggest box of chocolates in the world and dumped them on her lap.

It just made her cry all the more. Right now she valued her friends more than anything.

One hour later they were all gobsmacked. Emma slid her arm around her shoulders. 'Why didn't you tell us how you were feeling? You could have spent Christmas Day with any one of us.'

Grace shook her head. 'I didn't want to put a dampener on anyone else's Christmas.'

Sophie narrowed her eyes. 'But what about your Christmas? Finlay's certainly put a dampener on that.'

Grace sighed. 'It's not his fault I fell hook, line and sinker. I knew right from the start that he was a widower. I should have known better than to fall in love.'

Ashleigh leaned forward and slipped her hand into Grace's. 'But we can't always control where our heart will take us. Finlay took you to the staff party, he kissed you, he took you to Scotland, he slept with you. Then he took you to meet his family.' She shook her head and leaned back on her heels. 'It doesn't matter what way I look at this, Grace. He led you on. He didn't guard your heart the way he should have.'

'People don't always love you back,' Grace replied flatly.

Sophie slammed her hand on the table. 'Then the man's a fool.' She lifted her glass towards Grace. 'Whatever happens next, we're here for you, Grace. All of us. We're your family now.'

The words made her heart swell. She looked around at her friends with love and appreciation. 'Thank you, girls. That means so much. But I know what I need to do. I know how to take things forward for me.' She gave her head a shake. 'I don't need a man to determine what to do with my life. I have plans. I need someone who can stand by my side and support my choices in life. If Finlay can't do that—then he isn't the right man for me.' She lifted her glass to raise a toast then paused. Something sparked in her brain. She turned towards Sophie. 'Ashleigh said you went for drinks with some gorgeous Italian. I haven't heard about it yet. Spill.'

Anything to distract her from the way she was feeling right now.

Because one thing was for sure. The next steps would be the hardest.

He couldn't take it. He couldn't take it for a second longer. Four days were already four days too many.

He'd only needed one glimpse of Grace to know that this situation couldn't continue.

She was standing at the lifts with her cart, waiting to go upstairs. He walked over purposely and caught her by the elbow. 'Come with me for a second.'

'What?' She looked shocked. He'd caught her off guard.

He steered her towards one of the nearby empty rooms. 'We need to talk.'

She lifted her chin determinedly and folded her arms across her chest. 'Do we? I thought everything had been said.'

He ran his fingers through his hair and tried to find the right words. 'I hate seeing you like this.'

'Like what?'

'I hate seeing you so miserable—especially when I know it's all my fault.'

'I'm glad there's something we can agree on.' The words had obviously been on the tip of her tongue. She gave a little shake of her head. 'I'm a grown-up, Finlay. And so are you.'

He stepped closer. Her perfume drifted around him, giving him agonising flashbacks to the Christmas party and to Christmas night. 'Maybe we should have a rethink? Maybe, now that we're back, we could see each other when I'm back in London? I mean, I'm away a lot on business. But we could have drinks. Dinner.' He was rambling. Words were spilling out.

Her face paled. 'Tell me that you're joking?'

Not quite the effect he was looking for. 'Why?'

He could see the bottom edge of her jaw line tremble. It was something he'd never seen before in Grace Ellis. Rage.

'Why?' She shouted so loudly he winced. Guests in the bar next door would have heard.

She marched straight up under his chin, her eyes flashing madly. 'I'll tell you exactly why, Finlay Armstrong.' She pushed her finger into his chest. 'I am so much better than this.' She shook her head fiercely. 'I am not having a three-way relationship with a ghost. You can't move on because you won't let yourself. I don't want to spend my life living in the shadow of another woman. I don't deserve it and I don't need this. Don't come in here and offer me a tiny piece of yourself, Finlay. I don't want that. It's not enough. It will never be enough.' The fury started to dissipate from her voice. She took a step backwards. Her hand was shaking.

He saw her suck in a breath and pull herself back up. The expression in her brown eyes just about ripped out his soul. He'd tried to conjure up some remedy, some patchwork arrangement that might work. But his misplaced idea had backfired spectacularly.

'I want a change of shifts. I don't want to be around when you're here. I'm going to speak to Clio about a transfer. We work in the Corminster across town. I'll ask if I can do my shifts there instead.'

'What?' Panic gripped him like a hand around his throat.

Her eyes focused on the door. She started walking straight towards it. Her shoulders seemed straighter, her head lift stronger. 'You'll have my resignation in the morning. I'll make it official and keep everything above board.'

For the briefest of pauses her footsteps faltered. There was so much circulating in his head. This was exactly what he didn't want. This was the absolute opposite of what he wanted.

Grace's voice softened for a second. 'Goodbye, Finlay,' she said as she opened the door and left.

CHAPTER ELEVEN

HE'D BEEN ON the roof most of the night. It was Frank who finally found him.

'Mr Armstrong? What are you doing? Why—you're freezing.' Frank whipped off his jacket and put it around his shoulders.

He hadn't meant to stay up here so long. But the frustration in him had built so much that he'd punched a wall in the penthouse and knew he had to get outside and away from anyone. The roof had been the ideal solution. Too bad he hadn't thought to bring a coat.

One hand held the ceramic angel. He'd pushed it into his pocket when he'd closed up the house. The other hand held the silver heart from Mrs Archer. One symbolised a lost love, the other a new.

Looking out over the darkness of London, lit only by Christmas lights, had been haunting. Watching the sun start to rise behind Battersea Park and the Albert Bridge had been a whole new experience. It made him realise that the lights at Battersea Park should be purple instead of white and red. Purple seemed a much more festive colour.

Frank's fierce grip pulled him to his feet and over to the stairs. The heat hit him as soon as he stepped inside again. He hadn't realised he was quite so cold.

Frank walked him down to the penthouse and made a quick phone call. 'I've ordered you some breakfast and some coffee.' He paused. 'No, scrub that. Give me a second.' He picked up the phone again and spoke quietly before replacing it. 'I've ordered something more appropriate.' He walked over to the room thermostat and turned it up. He looked around the room, then left and scouted in the bathroom, coming back with a fleecy dressing gown that Finlay rarely wore. 'Here, put that on too. I'm going to deal with something else. But I'll be back up in ten minutes to check on you.'

Heat was slowly but surely starting to permeate his body. His fingers were entirely white with almost a tinge of blue. They were starting to tingle as they warmed up.

He was still staring at the Christmas decorations. He'd made so many mistakes. He just didn't know where to start to try and put them right.

He closed his eyes for a second, trying to wish away some of the things that he'd said. When Anna had died, he'd truly believed the biggest part of him had died too. It wasn't true. Of course it wasn't true. He just hadn't been able to face up to his grief.

Concentrating on business and only business had been his shield. His saviour. It had also been his vice.

He'd let relationships with friends deteriorate. He'd shunned any pity or sympathy. It was so much easier to shut himself off from the world. A wave of embarrassment swept over him as he realised he'd also shut out his mum, dad and sister.

His sister had got married two years ago. He hadn't participated at all. He'd hardly even been able to bear attending. The occasion when he should have been happy for his sister, and dancing her around the marquee floor, he'd spent nursing a whiskey at the bar.

Now, she was pregnant with her first child and clearly nervous. Had he even told her how delighted he was to be an uncle? How much he was looking forward to seeing her with her child in her arms?

What kind of a person had he become?

There was a ping at the door. Room service. The trolley was wheeled in. He lifted the silver platter. Pancakes, eggs and bacon. Unusual choice. He looked in the lower part of the trolley for the coffee.

But there was no coffee. Instead, there was a hot chocolate, piled high with cream and marshmallows and dusted with chocolate.

He sagged back into his chair. Frank. How did he know?

The first sip was all it took. Two minutes later he was tearing into the pancakes, eggs and bacon. He flipped open his computer and did a quick search, made a few calls.

Then he made another.

'Mum? Hi. Yeah… Yeah… I'm fine. Well, I'm not fine. But let me handle that. I wanted to ask a favour. How would you feel about supervising the staff from a cleaning and restoration company for me? They can be there on the sixth of January.'

It was amazing. Just one simple but major act

made him feel as though a huge dark cloud had been pushed off into the distance.

She spoke for a long, long time. Finlay knew better than to interrupt. He just gave the occasional, 'Yes…yes…yes…thanks…'

Her final words brought tears to a grown man's eyes. He put the phone back down as Frank came into the room.

The room seemed brighter, the early-morning sun sending a yellow streak across the room. Frank looked approvingly at the empty plate. 'Good, you've eaten. You're looking a bit more like yourself.' He bit his lip.

Finlay stood up. He wanted to shower and get changed. The more his head cleared, the stronger his heart pounded. For the first time in five years he had personal clarity. His business acumen had never been affected, but his own life?

It was time to finally get started.

Frank was still standing.

'What's wrong?'

'You have a guest. She wanted to leave something in your office. But I told her to come upstairs.'

Finlay caught his breath. Frank's face was serious. 'I'll take this,' he said briskly as he stepped forward for the empty tray. His face was impartial but his muttered words weren't. 'Don't you dare upset her. Just don't.'

Somehow he got the feeling that if he were the last man on a sinking ship right now, Frank wouldn't let him in the lifeboat. Frank's green coat disappeared.

There could only be one person that would cause this type of fatherly protection in Frank.

The heart that had already been pounding started to race to a sprint. 'Grace?'

He stuck his head out of the door. Grace was standing rigid, a white envelope clutched in one hand.

'Grace?'

Her steely gaze met his. He'd never seen her look quite so determined. His heart gave a little surge.

She straightened her shoulders. She was wearing a classy black wool coat, with an unusual cut. It emphasised her small waist. There were red skirts sticking out from the bottom of the coat and he could see the red collar at her neck.

But there was something else—a real assuredness about her. His heart swelled a little. Grace just got more spectacular every time he saw her.

She marched forward and thrust the envelope towards him. 'I just wanted to leave this for you, but Frank insisted I spoke to you. My resignation.'

It was as if all his best dreams and worst nightmares had decided to cram themselves into one hour of his life.

Grace's hair was styled a little differently and her lips were outlined in red.

She looked vaguely familiar and it took a few seconds to realise why. 'You look like Alice Archer,' he said quietly. His hand reached up to touch her hair but Grace flinched backwards. He swallowed. 'The only thing different is your hair colour. You look amazing, Grace.'

Her eyebrows shot up. 'Really?'

As he realised what he'd just said he gave a nervous laugh. 'I mean it, though. I do.'

She was still holding out the envelope towards him. She had her black leather gloves on that he'd bought her. He shook his head. 'I'm not taking it.'

Her brow furrowed. 'You have to. You can't stop me resigning.' His reaction seemed to spur her on. 'There's no way you can stop me. I've made plans. I'm transferring my shifts. I've enrolled at college to do interior design and Clio will give me shifts that suit. I'm moving on, Finlay. I'm not going to stay here and watch you walk about in a fog for the rest of your life.'

There were rosy spots on her cheeks. There was an edge of determination to her. He loved it. He loved everything about it.

He walked over and put his hands on her shoulders. 'Grace, that's the best thing I've heard this year. You will be a fantastic interior designer. You *are* a fantastic interior designer. I can't think of anything more perfect for you. But you don't need to leave here to do that.'

There was an almost startled expression on her face. 'Yes. Yes, I do. I can't be around you, Finlay. I *won't* be around you.'

His heart twisted inside his chest. 'Not even if I tell you that I love you? Not even if I tell you I've been a complete fool?' He stopped to draw breath. 'Grace, for the first time in years you've made me wake up and look around. I wasn't paying attention to life—oh, I thought I was, but not really, not the way I should have.' He ran his fingers through his hair. He wished he'd showered. He wished he'd changed out of the clothes he'd spent all night wearing on the roof. He put his hands on his hips. 'It wasn't just Drumegan Castle that I neglected. It was everything else too.'

'What does that mean?'

He reached out for her hands. 'It means everything, Grace. I think I have been ready to move on. The only person that hadn't acknowledged that was me.'

She shook her head as he clutched her hands even tighter.

'I'm sorry. I don't know how to do this any more. I've forgotten every rule of dating that I ever knew.' He pressed one hand against his heart. 'All I know is that ever since I met you, I've felt alive again. I've woken up and had something to look forward to. I'll never forget Anna, but, for a few days there, I felt guilty because I'd hardly thought about her at all. My mind was just filled with you, Grace. Every time you smiled, every time you winked at me, every time you looked sad. The way you loved Christmas. When you shared with me about your grandmother. But I looked at you, and your capacity to love, and wondered if I could ever meet that. Ever fulfil that for you.'

Grace blinked and licked her red lips. Her gaze

was steady. 'What are you doing, Finlay? Where has this come from?'

He laughed and pointed to his head. 'In here.' Then his heart. 'And in here. I spent most of last night sitting on the roof trying to get my head in order. You know, after a while, you start to think the Battersea Power Station lights should be purple.'

The edges of her lips curled upwards for a few seconds. 'But I still want everything. I don't want half a relationship. Anna's gone, Finlay. But I'm not. I'm here. I won't share. Not with anyone dead or alive.'

She was deadly serious. It was written all over her face and it just made his heart ache all the more for the pain he'd caused her. 'I love you, Grace Ellis. How long does it officially take people to fall in love? Can it happen in a few hours, a few days, a few weeks? Because that's what it feels like to me. I'm sorry for what I said in the helicopter. I'm sorry for what I suggested yesterday. I don't want just to see you now and then. I want to see you every single day.' He reached over and touched her cheek. 'Every single day for the rest of my life.'

Her eyes were wet. He could see her struggle to

swallow. 'I don't know, Finlay. I just don't know. You hurt me.'

His hands were shaking by now. 'I know. I'm sorry. I can't promise that I'm good at all this. But what I can promise is that every day, for the rest of my life, I'll try and show you how much I love you. How much you mean to me. Will you let me, Grace? Will you let me try?'

He pulled his hands back. He had to give her space. He had to respect her wishes. He'd already trampled all over her heart once.

She turned and looked out of the window, across the snow-dusted rooftops of London.

'How long were you up on that roof?'

'What?'

'How long were you up on that roof?'

He shook his head. 'I'm not sure. I went up to try and clear my head. It must have been the early hours. I was there until Frank found me this morning.'

'And you didn't freeze to death?'

He could see her watching his reflection in the glass. 'Not yet. There wasn't enough snow. And I didn't have anyone to make snow angels with. It didn't seem like the right place, or the right time.'

'How do I know any of this is true?'

He nodded and walked over to the kitchen counter. 'When I phoned my mother this morning about cleaning up the castle, she threatened me with grievous bodily harm if I came back to visit without you.'

She spun around. 'So, your mother wants you to date me?'

He smiled. 'No, my mother wants me to marry you. But I have to beg for forgiveness first.'

She sucked in a breath and pulled her hands around herself. She rocked back and forth a little. 'You're going to clean up the castle?'

He nodded. 'Starting January the sixth. Once it's clean, I will probably need to hire an interior designer to help me redecorate.' He raised his eyebrows. 'Can you think of anyone I might ask?'

She took a step closer to the counter. 'I might do. You should think about the person who thought purple was such a Christmas colour. She decorated one of the most exclusive hotels in London.' He nodded and smiled as she added, 'But I've heard she's expensive.'

He picked up the decorations from the counter top. 'There's one last thing I need to do. To make this official. To make this right.' He held out his hand towards her. 'Will you come with me?'

She looked at his hand for a second before finally reaching out and sliding her hand into his. He walked them over to the private elevator, pressing buttons to take them to the ground floor.

It was New Year's Eve. The hotel was busy with guests staying for the New Year's celebrations. Finlay ignored them all. He strode across the foyer with Grace's hand in his, only slowing down when they reached the main Christmas tree.

He took a deep breath. 'A few weeks ago you found something and set it on my pillow.' He pulled the ceramic angel from his pocket and lifted it, hanging it on the tree. 'You also remembered to bring it to Scotland with us.' He lifted his hand towards it. 'It's a memory. One that I will treasure and respect.' He pulled something else from his pocket. 'But I have another gift.' He nodded his head and smiled. 'This one was left in my office. It's from a mutual friend. Discreet. Knowledgeable. With more finesse in her little finger than I can ever hope to achieve in my life.' He lifted up the silver heart and hung it on the tree in front of them. 'Alice gave me this before we'd ever met. She knew before I did, before *we* did, the potential that was in the air.'

He spun the silver heart around so Grace could see the engraving.

She read it out slowly. *"'Memories are special in every single way, But new memories can be made every single day.'"* She gasped and put her hand to her mouth. 'Alice gave you that?'

He nodded as he turned Grace around and slid his arms around her waist.

'How do you feel about making some new memories, for The Armstrong, and for Drumegan Castle?'

She smiled and wound her arms around his neck. 'I think I might have to be persuaded.'

He caught the twinkle in her eye. 'And how might I do that?'

She laughed. 'I can think of a few ways.' Then stood on her tiptoes to whisper in his ear.

He picked her up and swung her around. 'Grace Ellis, we're in public!' He put her feet back on the floor. 'But we've got to start somewhere.'

And so he kissed her—again and again and again.

* * * * *

MILLS & BOON®
Large Print – April 2017

A Di Sione for the Greek's Pleasure
Kate Hewitt

The Prince's Pregnant Mistress
Maisey Yates

The Greek's Christmas Bride
Lynne Graham

The Guardian's Virgin Ward
Caitlin Crews

A Royal Vow of Convenience
Sharon Kendrick

The Desert King's Secret Heir
Annie West

Married for the Sheikh's Duty
Tara Pammi

Winter Wedding for the Prince
Barbara Wallace

Christmas in the Boss's Castle
Scarlet Wilson

Her Festive Doorstep Baby
Kate Hardy

Holiday with the Mystery Italian
Ellie Darkins

MILLS & BOON®
Large Print – May 2017

A Deal for the Di Sione Ring
Jennifer Hayward

The Italian's Pregnant Virgin
Maisey Yates

A Dangerous Taste of Passion
Anne Mather

Bought to Carry His Heir
Jane Porter

Married for the Greek's Convenience
Michelle Smart

Bound by His Desert Diamond
Andie Brock

A Child Claimed by Gold
Rachael Thomas

Her New Year Baby Secret
Jessica Gilmore

Slow Dance with the Best Man
Sophie Pembroke

The Prince's Convenient Proposal
Barbara Hannay

The Tycoon's Reluctant Cinderella
Therese Beharrie

0417 Rom LP

MILLS & BOON®

Why shop at millsandboon.co.uk?

Each year, thousands of romance readers find their perfect read at millsandboon.co.uk. That's because we're passionate about bringing you the very best romantic fiction. Here are some of the advantages of shopping at www.millsandboon.co.uk:

* **Get new books first**—you'll be able to buy your favourite books one month before they hit the shops

* **Get exclusive discounts**—you'll also be able to buy our specially created monthly collections, with up to 50% off the RRP

* **Find your favourite authors**—latest news, interviews and new releases for all your favourite authors and series on our website, plus ideas for what to try next

* **Join in**—once you've bought your favourite books, don't forget to register with us to rate, review and join in the discussions

Visit **www.millsandboon.co.uk**
for all this and more today!